DAWNDANCER

by

Kate Crozier

 New Generation **Publishing**

THANKS

I would like to thank first and foremost Evelyn Burges who taught me the healing dance. This is a real dance that has been performed for thousands of years and is still danced in some places. Without it, there would be no story.

Next, my grateful thanks to Evelyn again, and to Annie Lloyd, Margot Cooper and Bebe Swanson for reading the manuscript at various stages and for their valuable comments, also to Bebe for editing. Thanks, too, to Kaia, Alice and Jess for reading the manuscript and giving me insights into how young readers found the story.

Last, but by no means least, a very big thank-you to Diane Melanie for the cover design and maps.

Kate Crozier 2012

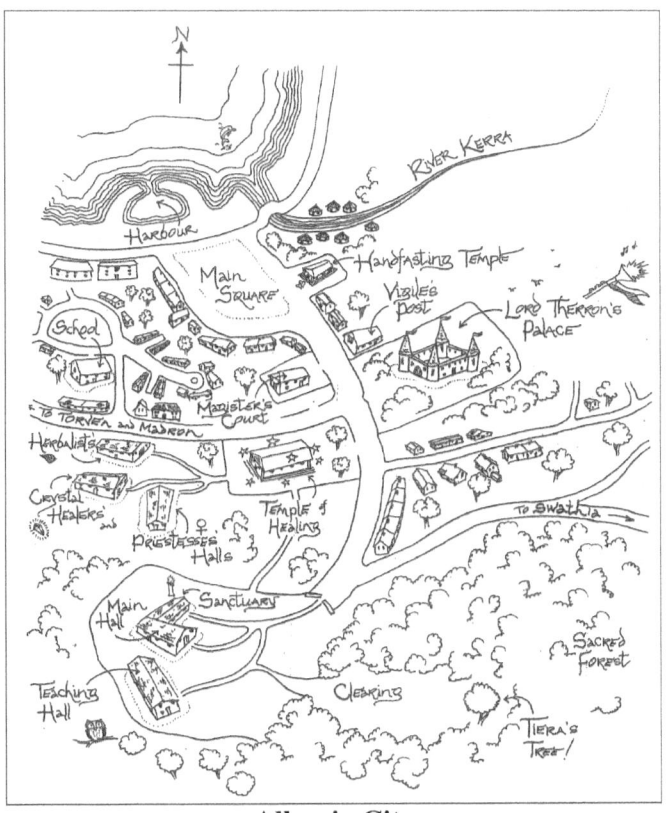

Allegria City

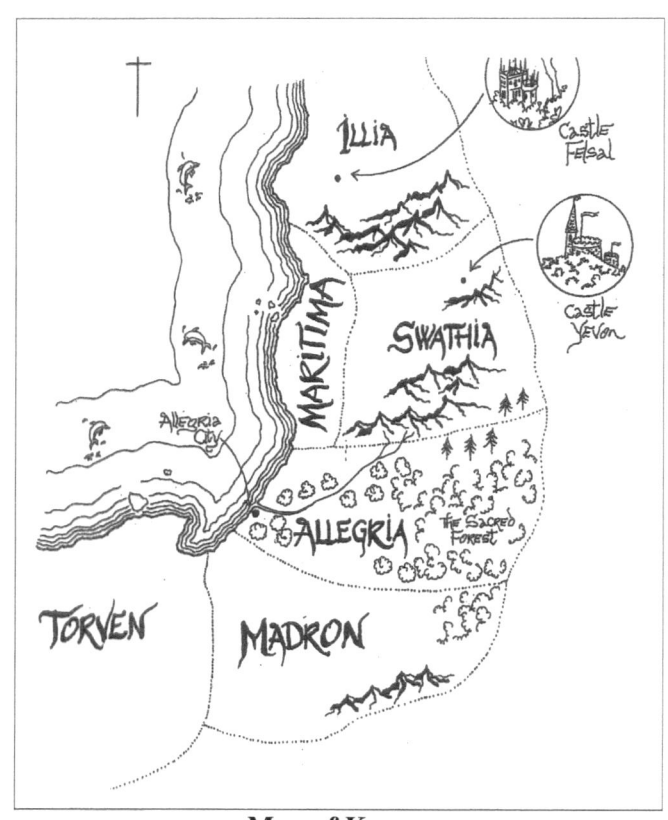

Map of Kerran

PEOPLE IN THE STORY

IN ALLEGRIA

Tiera	*Aged 12*
Hral	*Tiera's father*
Dilla	*Her sister, aged 9*
Frol	*Her brother, aged 6*
Fallod	*An elderly widower*
Beatta	*A Foster-mother*

Lord Therron	*Ruler of all Kerran*
Lady Helma	*His wife*
Lord Lars	*Governor of Madran*
Lady Nassia	*His wife*
Lord Radnel	*Governor of Torven*
Lady Fendra	*Governor of Maritima*

Guards, Vigiles, Priestesses, Servants, Townspeople.

AT DANCERS' HALL

Bryn	*A dance student, aged 13*
Selma	*" " " aged 12*
Crissa	*" " " aged 12*
Muria	*The First Dancer and head teacher*
Ruid	*Her second in command*
Allya	*A senior teacher*
Tama	*" " "*
Liana	*A dance teacher*
Cassie	*Matron at Dancers' Hall*
Minna	*Assistant to Cassie*
Nessa	*" " "*
Lyria	*A senior dance student*
Yssa	*A senior dance student*
Milon	*Yssa's twin brother*

Ambla, Arron, Breda, Emmi, Ferna, Gort, Grammi,
Gundra, Henga, Jekka, Juval, Kay, Nerron, Paphi,
Petra, Shali, Udi,Verla, Winna and Zorn
Dance students

IN ILLIA

Lord Felsal	*Governor of Illia*
Lady Bethna	*His wife*
Ildon	*Their infant son*
Torm	*A messenger*

IN SWATHIA

Lord Yevon	*Governor of Swathia*
Lady Khoda	*His wife*
Quar	*His steward*
Rhodi	*A footman*
Wilkin	*A miner, living on Lord Yevon's lands*
Ord	*A dwarf*
Gotti	" "
Nevo	" "
Druk	" "
Captain Kado	*A Captain of Guards*
Captain Brudo	" " " "
Jenk	*A Guard*

Servants, Dwarves, Guards, Stablemen

IN THE FOREST

The Lady Titania *Queen of the Fairies*
The Green Lord *(Sometimes called the Green Man)*
King of the Forest
Fairies, Elves, wild creatures, etc.

CHAPTER ONE

Tiera clung to the tree-trunk for dear life. She'd been perched on this branch all night, for fear of the animals that might be prowling the forest floor below her and she was hungry and tired and cold. But now it was dawn, and she would have started to climb down except that she'd seen a crowd of people moving into the clearing and she was afraid of being seen. If anybody spotted her now they might take her home, and that would be worse than if she'd never run away. She needed to get further away, a long way further, before she made any contact with people.

But now something was happening below her. A flute began to play a tune that made her shiver with delight and the people she had seen coming into the clearing started dancing. Tiera thought she had never seen anything so beautiful in all her life. There were men and women, young people and even children who looked younger than herself, all moving as if in a dream. They were leaping and stamping, gliding and spinning, sometimes all doing the same thing and sometimes alone or in twos or threes. In the centre of the group a silver haired woman seemed to float in the air. Tiera leaned forward to get a better view. Then she was falling, falling......

****

Bron and Selma reached the spot first.

"Here!" called Bron, "Over here! It's a girl, but she looks dead."

Selma was trying to pull twigs and thorns away from the limp little body.

Almost at once, Ruid was there, leaning over the child, feeling for a pulse. Selma and Bron stood back respectfully.

"No, she's alive," he smiled at them, "Let's get her into the clearing."

The crowd of dancers parted to make way for Ruid and his delicate burden, and by the time he reached the middle of the glade, three slender women were waiting, ready to ease the lifeless child from his arms and lay her gently on the mossy ground.

Ruid knelt down at her feet, the eldest of the women at her head, the other two on either side of her. Ruid placed his hands lightly on the child's feet, Muria, her silver hair tumbling over her face, put hers gently on either side of the girl's head, Tama and Allya on either side of her let their hands flutter just above the little body.

"No internal damage," said Ruid after a moment."

"Bruises, a lot of them, some fresh, a lot much older, said Tama.

"Some scratches and cuts, some old scars," reported Allya.

Muria took another moment or two before she said,

"Cold, hungry, scared: that's what I picked up first but there's a lot more going on deeper down. She's been unhappy for a long time and something's frightened her really badly more recently."

"Do you think we should revive her now, or get her back to the Hall first?" Ruid asked Muria.

"Let's get her into the Sanctuary before we wake her - that is, unless she comes round before that," she replied.

Ruid stood up and the women lifted the slight body and placed the girl carefully back in his arms. Muria turned to the dancers who were hovering anxiously nearby.

"Don't worry, the little girl is not seriously hurt. The bushes must have broken her fall. Ruid is taking her to the Sanctuary, and in any case it is time we all got back to the Hall for our Spring breakfast. You all behaved wonderfully, by the way. I'm proud of you for ending the dance as you did and then rushing to the rescue."

****

At the entrance to the Sanctuary Ruid called "Cassie, Nessa, Minna! Whoever's there. I've got an unconscious child here." Almost before he was inside a round, rosy woman came running to meet him.

"Oh! Who is it? What happened?"

"I don't know who she is. She literally fell out of a tree at the Spring rites." As he spoke, he laid the scrap of a girl on a couch. "We've scanned her. She doesn't have any serious injuries. Mostly shock and cold and some cuts and bruises."

Cassie bent over the child and smoothed the hair away from her forehead. As she did so, she saw the pale eyelids flutter. Then they opened, and Cassie was looking into huge, green eyes.

"Where am I?" the girl whispered, trying to sit up, "Who are you?"

"I'm Cassie, my chick. Don't be frightened now, nobody's going to hurt you. This gentleman's Ruid - he found you in the forest."

"Forest.....," the girl whispered, "forest," and closed her eyes again.

"Ruid, could you keep an eye on this little one while I make her a hot drink."

Ruid tried not to grin. A hot drink was Cassie's answer to every crisis! But he sat down next to the couch while Cassie bustled out.

"I'm Ruid. What's your name?"

"I'm Tiera," the child whispered.

"Tiera. That's a beautiful name. Where do you live? We should let your parents know that you are safe."

But the girl shook her head violently. She did not want to tell anybody where she had come from, in case they tried to take her back.

"Don't be afraid, Tiera. You don't have to tell me if you don't want to." Then they sat in silence until Cassie came back with a sweet-smelling drink.

"Here we are, chick. Drink up and you'll soon feel better."

Tiera sat up straight and took the mug. Despite its heat, she drained the sweet liquid almost in one go.

"My, you were thirsty! When did you last have a drink, my chick?" asked Cassie.

"I found a stream in the forest, I think it was yesterday."

"And what about food, my chick?"

"I picked some berries."

"And before that? When did you last have a proper meal?"

"Er, it was the day before that, before I ......" Tiera's voice trailed off.

"Right, my chick! I'm going to go and make you another drink and find something for you to eat," replied Cassie, then going to the door she called, "Nessa, Nessa, are you there? Come and look after a little girl for me for a few minutes."

A slender, dark haired young woman came running, wiping her hands on her apron as she hurried in. Ruid, seeing that Tiera was in good hands, said,

"I'd better go and tell Muria that the child's awake."

Before long, Cassie was back carrying a tray with another drink and a plate with a little cake and pieces of several different fruits delicately arranged on it.

"Here we are, my chick, you'll feel better when you've got a bit of breakfast inside you!" Cassie pulled a small table alongside the couch, put the tray on it and arranged cushions behind Tiera's back. As she did so, she noted how ingrained was the dirt on the child's arms and neck. This was not fresh dirt from a day or so spent in the forest. The same was true of her clothes. 'Well, there's a lot we don't know about her yet,' thought Cassie, 'but my guess is she's had a pretty tough life, poor little chick.'

Cassie left Nessa to watch over Tiera while she ate, but soon she was back again with a pile of clothes over her arm.

"Right, my chick, off to the bathtub with you! I've put some lovely oils in the water and Nessa will help you wash your hair. I've found some clothes that should fit you while I wash your things." She was far too kind to say that she thought the best place for Tiera's present clothing would be on a bonfire.

Nessa took Tiera along a corridor and opened a door. Tiera stared. She had never seen a bathing-room before. It was quite a simple room, with a white tub, pale blue tiles, some shelves and pale blue towels on a rail but to Tiera it was like something out of a dream. But she said nothing. She didn't want Nessa, or anybody, to think that she was ignorant, so she stepped into the wondrous place and sniffed at the fragrant water.

"I think Cassie has put lavender and one or two other things in the water," said Nessa, "Now, I'll leave you to bathe, and I'll come back in a little while to help you wash your hair."

"Thank you," said Tiera and when Nessa had gone she peeled off her torn clothes and put one foot tentatively in the water. It was hot, but not too hot, so she climbed in very carefully, holding on tight to the side of the tub, and even more carefully sat down. It took her several minutes to get used to the feel of hot water against her skin but finally she sighed and sank down until only her head was above water. It felt so wonderful, so comforting she closed her eyes and lay there, breathing in the sweet scents.

All of a sudden, she wanted to cry. She remembered when her mother was still alive, how she had taken her to the river every day and washed her with sweet soap. The river water was cold but the soap smelt like the water she was lying in now. Since her mother died, Tiera had taken Dilla and Frol to the river to bathe as often as she could but mostly they had to wash under a trickle of water from the pump that they shared with five other households. In hot weather, the pump often dried up, and it was a long time since they'd had any soap.

Thinking of soap, she remembered that she was supposed to be washing herself. She sat up, wiped her tears, took the fat bar of soap that sat on the side of the tub and began to lather herself. She'd just finished when Nessa tapped on the door.

"Can I come in?" she called.

"Yes," called back Tiera.

"Would you like me to scrub your back before I wash your hair?"

"Oh, yes please."

As Tiera bent forward Nessa had to stifle a gasp of shock: the girl's back was marked with fresh weals and old scars from many whippings as well as a host of bruises. Nessa said nothing, but made a mental note to report this to Cassie as soon as possible. Rather than scrub, she washed Tiera's back as gently as she could; even so, she felt the girl wince more than once. Then she turned to the matter of washing Tiera's hair. As she lathered and rinsed the tangled locks, another surprise awaited her, but a pleasant one this time; rinsing away the murky suds she realised that Tiera's mousey hair was, in fact, an exquisite silvery-gold.

"Now, I'll leave you to get dry and dressed - the clothes Cassie sorted out for you are over here - and then if you'd like to come back to the room we were in earlier, I'll dry your hair and brush it for you."

"Thank you," said Tiera as Nessa left, then she clambered out of the tub rather reluctantly, but drying herself on big, fluffy towels was another new pleasure, and then there were the fresh clothes to put on.

Dressed in new underwear, a tunic of some silky, silvery-grey material with a matching belt and soft leather sandals, she made her way back to where Nessa was waiting for her.

"My goodness, you look a real little dancer!" exclaimed Nessa before setting about brushing the tangles out of her hair. Before she'd finished, Cassie arrived with another drink and a snack for Tiera.

"Little and often, my chick, that's the way to eat when you haven't had a proper meal for a while. Eat up and when Nessa's finished with your hair, I'll take you to see Muria, she's waiting to talk to you. Muria's the First Dancer and the head teacher."

Tiera nodded but said nothing. She didn't like the idea of a talk, especially with somebody who sounded so important - it would doubtless involve questions about what she was doing in the forest and where she'd come from. Her biggest fear was that these people would take her home. That would be even worse than if she had not run away in the first place. Her father would beat her harder than ever and then he would make her marry Fallod. Fat, ugly old Fallod.

****

Muria's study was a light airy room. There were comfortable-looking seats, piles of cushions, soft rugs, flowers on a low table and windows opening onto a long lawn.

"Hello Tiera. You look much better than when I first saw you!" smiled Muria, "I can see that Cassie has been looking after you."

Muria's voice was so gentle, her smile so kind that Tiera's fear began to melt.

"Oh yes, she has been very kind," she said.

Muria held out her hand to Tiera and invited her to sit down. Tiera chose a seat near the window. At the back of her mind was the thought that if this lady wanted to send her back to her father, she could run.

"Tiera," Muria said softly, "I think you have had a very difficult life. Would you like to tell me about it?"

This took Tiera by surprise. She did not know that Cassie had reported the pitiful state of her back, still less that Muria had glimpsed some of her memories when she lay unconscious in the forest clearing, but she felt at once that she could tell her everything.

So she poured out the whole story: how her mother had died four years ago, how she had looked after her little brother and sister since then and done the housework, washed their few clothes and cooked whatever food she could scrape together. She told how her father came home drunk more and more often, how he beat her if his meal wasn't ready or she spoke too loudly for his fancy, in fact for any reason or none at all.

Muria leaned forward and took both of Teira's hands in her own.

"So you ran away?"

Tiera nodded. "I thought about for a long time, but I didn't want to leave Dilla and Frol. They're too little to look after themselves and I was afraid my father would start beating them as well. But then he said I'd got to marry Fallod. Fallod promised him a lot of money. Fallod's ugly, he's fat and he's older than my father, but when I cried and begged my father not to make me marry him, he beat me more than ever."

"Tiera, how old are you?" Muria asked.

"I'm twelve. I'll be thirteen in the winter.

"That's too young to get married," Muria said.

"Yes, that's why I ran away. I hid in the forest for two days - at least, I think it was two days - I hid in a tree at night, and then I saw you dancing and that's the last thing I remember."

Muria smiled. "I can tell you what happened next: you fell out of the tree. Bron and Selma found you lying unconscious in the bushes and thought you were dead, but Ruid ran after them, saw that you were alive and carried you back here. You woke up in Cassie's room and the rest, of course, you know." She did not mention how she, Ruid, Allya and Tama had scanned Tiera's body for injuries; there would be time enough for the child to learn about that aspect of the Dancers' work later. Then she went on:

"Later today, we are going to perform a Healing Dance for you. It is one of our duties as Dancers and it will help all your bruises and other hurts. Until then, I'm going to ask some people your own age to show you around Dancers' Hall." She rang a little bell, and soon a tall young woman appeared at the door.

"Minna, would you go and find Bron for me, and Selma, and tell them to come to my study? No, no, they haven't done anything wrong! I have a little job for them to do, that's all."

Soon Minna came back with two younger people. As they came into the room, Bron exclaimed "Wow!" then clamped his hand over his mouth, embarrassed, but Muria smiled.

"Yes, Tiera looks rather different from the girl you found a few hours ago!

Now, as you two were the first to find her, I thought you should be the ones to show her around Dancers' Hall. Bring her back in time for lunch."

CHAPTER TWO

The three young people stepped out of Muria's windows onto the lawn.

They stood awkwardly for a moment, taking each other in. Selma, Tiera noticed, was taller than herself and, she guessed, roughly the same age. Her brown eyes twinkled with mischief and Tiera decided at once that she would love to have Selma as a friend. Bron was a head taller, fair haired, tanned, serious looking.

"What would you like to see first?" he asked.

Tiera shook her head: she didn't know what the choices were.

"Let's start with the Teaching Hall," suggested Selma, "There won't be any classes going on right now, everybody will be at break."

So they turned left and took the short path leading to a large building with huge windows, stretching almost from floor to ceiling. Most of the ground-floor windows stood open to the lawns in front of them.

"This is where we have our dance classes," said

Selma, "When the weather is good we often come out on to the lawn to practice. Oh, take your shoes off before we go inside!" They all unbuckled their sandals and dangled them from their hands as they went in, through an entrance hall and into a large airy room where various musical instruments stood in one corner; drums, a lyre and cases containing Tiera knew not what. She gazed at the pale wood floor, the high ceiling, the curtains dyed in delicate rainbow shades, the sheer size of it all for she had never been inside such a large room in all her life and was as amazed as she had been by the bathing-room a little earlier.

"Oh, this is so beautiful!' she sighed.

"Yes, it's quite new," said Bron, "It was only built two years ago in honour of the five hundredth anniversary of Dancers' Hall, though there were obviously dancers before that - they just weren't organised into a Hall before."

Selma, bored with Bron's little history lesson, moved away and began to repeat some dance steps she had been learning that morning, humming the tune as she did so.

"Oh, do that again!" said Tiera, and Selma complied. This time Tiera tried to copy her.

"Hey! That wasn't bad Tiera," said Bron, "Have you done much dancing before?"

"No, never."

"Well, that was jolly good for a first try."

Tiera blushed, but then they moved on to look at the other rooms. There were three more dance rooms on the ground floor - so that several classes could practise at the same time, Selma explained, then they went upstairs to look at the other classrooms. Tiera was, once again, entranced by everything but to Selma and Bron it was simply the place where they did the more boring lessons, the ones that didn't involve dancing! They didn't know that Tiera had never been to school, had never seen a perfectly ordinary classroom and they would have hurried on if she had not stopped and asked so many questions. In the last room there was a large, colourful chart on one wall which fascinated her, and she pored over the pictures for what seemed ages.

"What is this all about?" she asked.

"One Thousand Years of Kerran History" said Bron,

reading out the heading written across the top of the chart in a mock-pompous voice, and was on the point of adding "Can't you read?" when he realised that would be very rude. Instead, he came and stood next to Tiera and pointed out the most important features:

"This picture is of the Lords of the Six Provinces signing the treaty that created Kerran. Before that, they were all squabbling with each other. And this is the building of the Temple of Healing, and this last picture is the very first Dancers' Hall - pulled down a long time ago. Well, it was built five hundred years ago as I said just now so it would have been pretty grotty by now!" He moved further along the wall where there wee some other pictures "Look, this one is of Lord Therron laying the foundation stone of this building a couple of years ago, so that brings us pretty well up to date as we are in 1503 now."

"Oh, you and your history!" said Selma, "I reckon we should show Tiera the main Hall if we're to be finished by lunchtime. She's seen some of the Sanctuary already and we're not allowed into the rest of it without permission."

As they retraced their steps across the lawn, Tiera asked suddenly,

"Who was the silver haired lady who was dancing with you this morning?"

"That must have been Muria. There's nobody else with silver hair among the Dancers," answered Bron.

"No, it wasn't Muria. I know who she is now. It was somebody else. She was dancing with a man in green. His clothes looked as if they were made of leaves."

Bron looked at Selma and raised his eyebrows. Selma, dropping back a step so that Tiera couldn't see her, put her fingers on her lips.

"Later!" she mouthed silently, then in a normal voice, "This is where we live," as they went in the main entrance of the Hall.

"The dorters and the students' sitting rooms are upstairs, the refectory and the kitchens are downstairs, and some of the adult Dancers have apartments here. Most of the teachers live in the Hall. Some of the others do, too, but some of them live in the town and come here for classes and so on."

"Classes?" queried Tiera, "Why do grown-up

dancers come to classes? Surely they know how to do it already?"

Bron and Selma both burst out laughing.

"Dancers have to keep in training," explained Bron. "They need to come to classes every day to keep their muscles and everything in condition. We don't only dance in a dance class; we do exercises to make our bodies ready for dancing."

"They have to learn new dances, too, just like we do, " said Selma, "There's always something new going on."

Tiera realised that there was a great deal she did not know about this new world that she had stumbled across, but she ached to know more. She would have bombarded her companions with more questions, but Selma was saying,

"Come on, I'll show you my dorter - Bron, see you back here in a bit."

By the time they had explored Blue dorter and the girls' sitting room Selma realised that it was time to take Tiera back to Muria, so they ran down the stairs - strictly forbidden, Selma grinned over her shoulder -

found Bron and made their way back to Muria's study.

"Tiera, do you feel brave enough to have lunch in the refectory with everybody else?"

Tiera nodded. She was not sure if she wanted lunch after all Cassie's feeding during the morning but the prospect was too exciting to refuse.

"Then we'll all go together, and you can sit at Selma's table."

Muria led Tiera by the hand until they reached a platform at the far end of the refectory where four people were sitting at a long table. Tiera recognised one of them as the man who had been in Cassie's room with her that morning. Muria led her up the steps, then clapped her hands for silence and said:

"Dancers, this is Tiera, who arrived so dramatically in our midst this morning! Happily, she was not badly hurt and she's going to share our mid-day meal. I just ask you not to pester her with too many questions all at once and let her eat in peace." She bent down to speak to Tiera again and pointed to the table where Selma had saved a seat for her, "Go and enjoy your meal now, and come back to me when you've finished."

Looking down at the long tables as Muria spoke, Tiera realised that almost everybody was wearing exactly the same clothes as herself. Suddenly she understood what Nessa's had meant earlier that morning when she said that Tiera looked 'a real little dancer' and in that moment, she knew, without a single doubt, that that was what she wanted to be. A real dancer.

She was surprised to find that she did, in fact, have an appetite for lunch, though the girls around her did not take much notice of Muria's request.

"Oh, shut up all of you! Leave her alone," said Selma, after a while.

"Goody two-shoes!" sneered a girl a few seats away, "I suppose because you got to her first you think you're in charge?"

"Yes I do!" retorted Selma, "Muria asked me look after Tiera, so you can just mind your own business Crissa."

But now chairs were being scraped back and people were beginning to leave. Muria caught Tiera's eye and beckoned her to come back to the platform.

"Tiera, you've already met Ruid who is Second Dancer, but I'd like you to meet Tama and Allya who are both senior Dancers and teachers. Later this afternoon, as I told you, we are going to perform a Healing Dance for you and I think you'll feel happier if you've met all the people who are going to be involved."

Tiera smiled shyly and held out her hand to the two women, who shook it in turn: first Tama, tiny and compact, with corn coloured hair spilling out of the knot she had tied it in; then Allya, very tall, long-legged, like a gazelle, her eyes were like a gazelle's too, nut brown like her hair. She was almost as tall as Ruid, who hovered behind her. He smiled at Tiera, friendly lines crinkling round his grey eyes and she noticed that there was just a little bit of grey at his temples too, though most of his hair was black.

"All four of us have classes to teach now," said Muria, "so I think it best if you go back to Cassie's room and rest until somebody fetches you."

****

Tiera woke with a start. 'Where am I?' she thought, then looking around Cassie's room it all began to come back to her, all the events of this strange day. And there were still more to come. She hadn't meant to go to sleep. She'd just lain down on the couch for a little while after the noisy lunch and now shadows were lengthening in the room.

She stood up and went to the window. Little groups of girls and boys were playing on the grass outside: here and there lone individuals sat reading. In the distance some livelier souls were playing a ball game. She heard a door open behind her and turned to see Nessa.

"Tiera, it's time for your healing," she said softly, "Come with me and I'll take you to the Inner Sanctuary."

They went along a corridor, up some stairs and along another corridor.

Nessa knocked at a door and said,

"Tiera is here."

"We are ready for her. Please bring her in."

The room was lit by the late afternoon light, filtering though gauzy curtains at the huge windows, and the many candles that flickered on every side, their flames reflecting off the myriad surfaces of a large purple crystal that stood on a sconce to one side. The walls were painted a delicate shade of mauve, and at the far end of the room stood Muria, Allya, Tama and Ruid, each dressed in different shades of mauve or purple.

Tama and Allya came forward and, taking Tiera's hands, led her to a low couch in the centre of the space. Once she had lain down, they covered her with a lilac silk shawl. Now Muria gave a signal and a side door opened. In came a man who Tiera had seen that morning playing the flute in the forest clearing, and after him came a dozen young dancers, all in mauve robes, who took up their positions round the room.

Softly, very softly, the flute began to play and the dancers slowly circled the room making formal patterns with their arms. Gradually they came closer to Tiera until they surrounded the couch. Their hands hovered over her as they moved their arms from side to side. It looked to Tiera almost as if they were pulling something out of the air around her and discarding it behind them. Now the four First Dancers stepped into the centre of the circle and began a similar dance, though now it seemed they were putting something into the air.

The music grew faster, the dancers with it. Tiera could not keep her eyes open any longer, but she felt the air swirling as the dancers swept around her, she sensed their hands fluttering over her body, she heard the pad of their feet on the floor, faster and faster, wilder and wilder, until the music slowed and hushed and the feet with it.

Then there was a silence deeper than anything Tiera had known in her life. Utter stillness.

After a long time, she opened her eyes. The dancers stood and knelt like statues in the darkened room. She did not know how long they had been like that. All she knew was peace. A great wave of happiness swept over her. Then she closed her eyes again and slept.

CHAPTER THREE

They were gathered in Cassie's cosy room: the four teachers and Cassie herself. Spicy aromas came from the jug she had just brought in.

"I thought a little mulled wine would be a good idea!" she said as she poured, "I've been in and put a quilt over the little one. I think she'll sleep all night now."

Muria nodded, "Yes, we did weave a sleep magic for her at the end. A long sleep will help her to absorb the healing."

"What are we going to do about her?" asked Ruid. "We clearly can't send her back to her father."

"No, that's certain," said Allya, "Do you think we should report him to the authorities? Beating her, trying to sell her, it's all against the law."

"Certainly, but we don't even know where he lives. Tiera's very vague about where her home was. A slum near the river is all I could gather. She was terrified of being sent back there."

"We couldn't do that, after all you've told us!" said Allya, "but then, what else can we do? We can hardly keep her here."

"Why not?" asked Muria, very quietly.

"Well, what would we do with a child who is not a dance student? How would she fit in?"

"And suppose she *were* a dance student? It is what she wants with all her heart. I picked it up loud and clear in the refectory today, and again during the healing dance."

The others were silent. Muria, they knew, had the greatest powers of them all when it came to hearing other people's thoughts. It could be awkward at times! But Muria was speaking again.

"There are one or two things more I should tell you about Tiera. Bron and Selma came to me after lunch and told me firstly that she had copied Selma dancing in one of the practice halls as accurately as if she'd been training for several years. Secondly, they think she saw the Lady Titania during this morning's Rites."

The others gasped.

"Yes, she asked them who was the silver-haired lady dancing with us, and when they said Muria, she replied that she knew who I was and it was not me. She added that the silver-haired lady was dancing with a man in dressed green leaves."

"The Green Lord! You think she has the Sight?" asked Tama.

"Either that or........ Have you noticed her hair? Have you looked at her eyes?"

"Emerald green," said Cassie, who had been the first to look into them when Tiera woke from her faint, "and that shimmery gold hair. Oh my! You think she's a half-fay?"

"I think it's a possibility."

"Well, you certainly know better than any of us," said Cassie, looking into Muria's own green eyes. Cassie had known Muria longer than anybody in Dancers' Hall, and remembered when her hair, too, shone like spun gold.

"I have an idea how it might be managed, but I'm too tired to think it through in detail," said Muria, "In the morning I shall put my mind to it and see what might be done. Now I'm going to bed."

****

The four teachers gathered in Muria's apartment to share breakfast and discuss what was to be done about Tiera.

"Well, I confess I have had a sleepless night thinking about our little foundling!" laughed Muria, "but I have come up with a plan that I think might work. Let me outline it for you, and see if you agree."

The others nodded.

"Right. I suggest that we start by trying Tiera in the beginners class with the day students and ....."

"But she'll be four or five years older than them," protested Allya,

"I can't see it working. Surely she'd be embarrassed and miserable dancing with seven and eight year olds?"

"If she feels as strongly about becoming a dancer as my reading of her suggests, I think she'd be willing to put up with that for a while. We'd move her up through the classes as quickly as possible."

41

Allya still looked doubtful, though Ruid nodded thoughtfully.

"What about lessons other than dancing?" asked Tama, "We don't know whether she's had any schooling at all, though it sounds unlikely."

"We'd have to find out," agreed Muria, "and we may need to adopt the same tactics there as well."

"It *might* just work," said Ruid, "but I think it would be important for her to spend as much time with her own age-group as possible."

"Of course. I'd need to talk to Cassie about dorter arrangements but it would be easy enough for Tiera to eat with her peers, use the same sitting-room and so forth."

"I'm not convinced," said Tama, "but I suppose we could try. It would depend on Tiera herself - how badly she wanted to be a dancer."

"Unless my reading of her is wildly wrong, I can assure you she wants it more than anything else on earth," said Muria "but after breakfast I will ask her in person and take it from there."

Allya said nothing as they dispersed, but she had an uncomfortable feeling that Muria knew perfectly well she did not like the idea at all.

****

When Tiera woke the sun was pouring through the gauze curtains. She looked round the peaceful room, remembered last night's dance and sighed with happiness. She stretched luxuriously and realised that her body felt different. It didn't hurt, not anywhere! She could scarcely remember a time when she had not hurt somewhere or other - perhaps a long time ago when she was little and her mother was still alive. She lay on her back for a while, enjoying the sensation, until there came a soft tap on the door, and Nessa's voice whispering,

"Are you awake?"

"Yes, come in."

"Hello! Did you sleep well? Cassie's busy and she's asked me to look after you this morning. You know the way to the bathing-room now, don't you? I'll go and

43

make you some breakfast, and after that, Muria wants to see you again."

As she made her way to the bathing-room, Tiera thought it was only yesterday when she'd been scared of talking to Muria. Now she looked forward to it! She undressed and looked at her back in the mirror. However much she twisted and turned her head, she could not see a bruise or a scar anywhere.

****

"Sit down, Tiera," said Muria, "I've been thinking very hard about your future but I'd like to know what you think. I can't imagine you want to go back to your father, so what do you want to do instead?"

"I want to be a Dancer." She looked anxiously at Muria, fearing that she'd been presumptuous.

"Good! That's what I thought you would say."

Tiera stared at the First Dancer. She hadn't said it was impossible!

"It won't be easy," Muria went on, "Dancers usually begin training when they're about 8 years old. You'd have to work very hard to catch up."

"Oh! I'll work very, very hard. I promise. I'll do anything I have to do to be a dancer. Ever since I saw you all dancing in the forest I've wanted to do the same."

"So much so that you forgot to hang on to your tree!" laughed Muria, "Well, this is what I propose..." and she set out the plan she had described to the younger teachers. By the time she had finished, Tiera's eyes were sparkling.

"When can I start?"

"The beginners' class is not until later in the afternoon. The younger children live in the city with their families and come here for their dance lessons after they have finished school for the day. Students come to live here when they are about ten years old, and then only if we can see that they are likely to be a good dancer at the end of the training."

"Suppose you don't think I'll be a good dancer?"

"We'll worry about that if it happens. Now, you'll need to talk to Cassie about all sorts of things, such as clothes and where you will sleep. Can you find your way back to her?"

"Yes, I think so."

"Then off you go."

Tiera floated out of the study on a cloud and raced across the lawns to the Sanctuary. It took her some time to find Cassie, but when she did, and poured out her news in a torrent, Cassie said,

"Well, that's wonderful my chick. Let's go and sort out some clothes while I think about which dorter we might fit you into."

She led Tiera to a room lined with cupboards and said,

"Now, let's see, you'll need another set of day clothes, a couple of nightgowns, bathrobe, undies, tunics for your dance classes, a cloak for out of doors .... I think I can find most of that for you. We can see about winter clothes later on." She opened and shut cupboards, rummaged through shelves until she had amassed what looked to Tiera like enough clothes for five or six people.

"Well, my chick, that was easy enough, but I'd better have a think about where you're to sleep. Let's go and have a nice hot drink while I sort something out."

Back in her room, Cassie took out a large chart and studied it.

"Now, there's an empty bed in Pink dorter, but the girls in there are all younger than you. There's a space in Green, but I'd rather pop you into Blue. Selma's in Blue, and she's about the only person you've got to know yet, isn't she? Right! I've got it. Crissa isn't very popular with the other girls in Blue, but she's got friends in Green. I'll switch her over, which will make her happy and leave a space for you, all in one go." Cassie was clearly pleased with this solution, and gathered up most of the pile of new clothes.

"Right, chick, if you pick up the rest of those things and follow me, we'll go and sort you out a little space of your own."

****

The time came for Tiera's first dance class and she waited anxiously outside the practice rooms. Then

Muria came hurrying from the neighbouring room where she had been teaching and said,

"Let's go and find your teacher."

In the classroom, Muria introduced Tiera to a slender, red-haired woman with a mass of freckles and a turned-up nose who Tiera remembered seeing in the forest clearing.

"Liana, this is Tiera who I spoke to you about earlier. Tiera, this is Liana who looks after our beginners. I shall leave you in her good hands."

Liana took Tiera's hand and welcomed her, but by now other children were filtering into the room and as soon as they were all assembled, she introduced Tiera to the class. Seeing that they were all staring at Tiera, she laughed and said,

"Don't stare! You know it's ill mannered. Yes, I know Tiera is older than any of you but there are reasons why she didn't start dancing sooner. Now Tiera, for today I think you'd better join the boys in the back row. That way you can follow what the girls in front are doing".

The flautist who sat at one side of the room began to

play. First they practised the correct way to stand, then how to hold their arms, moving them from one position to another in time to the music. Tiera watched the girls in front and copied everything they did. From time to time, Liana corrected one of them or came to Tiera to move a hand or turn her head, each time with some encouraging words. Then came walking in time to the music, then running, skipping and back to walking. Finally, Liana asked the flautist to play something for them to make up their own dances. Tiera thought this the best part of the lesson but the whole hour passed so quickly that she was amazed when it was time to bow to Liana at the end.

She made her way back to Blue dorter to change, only getting lost once en route. Elated by her first experience of dancing, she arrived on the top floor in an exuberant mood, only to find the dark-haired girl who had been rude to Selma at the lunch table stamping and throwing clothes about - Tiera's clothes, she realised.

"Oh, here you are. Little Miss Precious herself. You think you can just waltz in here and take over my place, do you?" as she threw a sandal at Tiera as hard as she could.

"Stop it, Crissa, stop it. It's not Tiera's fault if Cassie's decided to put her in here," cried Emmi, trying to grab Crissa's arm, but Crissa shook her off and turned on her.

"Oh, you're going to take her side as well, are you?" She turned and picked up another sandal but just as she threw it, Cassie came through the door.

"Lucky for you that didn't hit anybody, my girl," she said. "It's coming to something when Jekka has to come and fetch me because you're creating such a rumpus. Now, you will pick up Tiera's clothes, put them back where they belong and come with me to Green dorter." Cassie sat down heavily on the end of a bed and folded her arms, "And hurry up. I haven't got all day."

"Oh, please! I'll go and sleep in Green dorter," said Tiera, "I don't want to upset anybody."

"You'll stay right here, chick," said Cassie, "It's up to me to say who sleeps where, and the truth is that Crissa will be happier in Green once she's stopped showing off."

Sulkily, Crissa picked up the scattered garments and put them back on the bed that was now Tiera's. Cassie stood up, took her arm and marched her out of the room.

CHAPTER FOUR

By the end of a week, Liana reported that Tiera could do everything that was taught in the beginners' class, and she was moved up to the next group, exchanging her yellow sash and hair band for pale blue ones. Liana was still her teacher, for this class followed on when the beginners' ended. Now she learned how to put foot positions and arm positions together, some simple steps and a whole series of exercises designed to make her stronger, more supple, more agile. There were musical exercises too; repeating a rhythm that Liana clapped, for example, or humming a tune after the flautist. Tiera loved every minute of every lesson.

Crissa, passing her in a corridor after her class, smiled acidly and said "Oh Tiera, it must be *such* fun dancing with the tinies!"

Tiera looked her straight in the eye and replied,

"As a matter of fact, it is!"

But dance classes only took up an hour of each day and other lessons were a very different matter; Tiera's mother had taught her to read and write a little, but that was all and there were no classes suitable for her. Muria found some simple books for her and the teachers coached her when they were not taking classes, but they had their regular duties and those times were brief.

One afternoon Bron found her crying in the gardens.

"Hey, Tiera, what's the matter?"

"These wretched books, my sums, everything. Why do I have to know all this stuff when I just want to be a dancer? What's any of it got to do with dancing?"

"Not a lot!" he agreed, "but we all have to do it. Poor old Tiera, it must be really tough for you, though." He gave her a friendly hug and said "Come on, let's sit down and see if I can help a bit.

After that Bron, Selma, Ambla and the other girls from Blue dorter took it in turns to read with Tiera every day. Tiera gritted her teeth and practised writing and sums when everybody else was in lessons, and at last the time came when she was able to join the ten-year old's classes, even though it was sometimes a struggle to keep up.

But the dance classes made it all worthwhile. She moved steadily upwards through the classes, swapping her blue sash for a pink one, the pink one for green until she was working with the ten-year olds who hoped soon to become boarders. Allya taught this class, and although she had initially doubted the wisdom of Muria's plans for Tiera, she had grown fond of the girl and saw that she did, indeed, have the makings of a dancer.

The day came when they would learn who had been chosen to move into the next class. Everybody was edgy and tense that day, tempers frayed and petty squabbles broke out for no real reason but finally, the moment arrived. Muria, Tama and Ruid joined Allya at the end of the class, and most of the day students' parents crowded into the room to hear the decisions.

Muria unrolled a long list and began to read:

"Arron, Gort, Juval and Udi are chosen from among the boys and, from the girls, Grammi, Gundra, Petra, Shalli and Zora. They will move into Dancers' Hall and begin their full-time training as Novices. Then, as most of you know, Tiera is already living at Dancers' Hall but she will now move into the next class and begin full-time training with the rest of this group."

Clapping broke out all round, boys slapped each other on the shoulders, girls hugged each other or burst into tears but Muria continued.

"These have not been easy decisions to make. This is an unusually gifted group, and after a lot of discussion between Allya, Tama, Ruid and myself, we made the final choice mainly on the basis of age and physical maturity. In other words, the older boys and girls and those who are tall for their age will go into the next class and live in Hall. The rest of you, don't give up hope! There isn't a single boy or girl in this class who hasn't got the potential to be a dancer, we want you all to continue and we will review your progress later in the year. In other words, we are not turning anybody ....."

Nobody heard any more for the cheering and clapping and jumping up and down. As for Tiera, she thought her heart would burst with joy. Ever since she came to Dancers' Hall the fear that she would not be good enough had always been in the back of her mind and with it, anxiety about what would happen to her if she was not.

Back in Blue dorter her friends hugged her, squeezed her, congratulated her over and over again.

"Bravo!" cried Emmi.

"I knew you could do it!" said Selma.

"Now you're really one of us!" said Jekka.

"Oh, thank you, thank you," said Tiera, almost in tears, "but you know I'll still have to work very hard. I'm two years behind all of you in my dance class and everything else."

"Oh, knowing you, you'll have caught up with us in a couple of weeks!" joked Ambla.

****

The following week, the nine boys and girls chosen from her class moved into the Hall, and there was a little ceremony to welcome them, in which Tiera was included because she was about to become a Novice, too. Afterwards, Muria talked to them about their future lives as Dancers.

"The first duty of a Dancer," she began, "is to serve the Temple of Healing. One day, some of you may even choose to become Temple Priests or Priestesses, but all of us dance in the Temple on the feast days, and perform healing dances elsewhere whenever needed. Our second duty is to celebrate the changing seasons, both in public ceremonies and privately in the Sacred Forest."

Tiera smiled a private smile, remembering how she had first seen the Dancers at dawn on the first day of Spring, but Muria was going on.

"We act as intermediaries between the forest creatures and the rest of the world. Our Hall was built between the city and the Sacred Forest for that reason. Apart from that, we're often asked to dance at handfastings, namings and other ceremonies. These are not duties - we get paid to dance - but these occasions are very important to the people involved so we prepare and perform just as earnestly as for our sacred duties. But, above all, we dance because we love to!"

Now Tiera's life changed almost overnight; there was a dance class first thing every morning, normal "school" classes to follow and another dance class in the afternoon. These afternoon classes were what Tiera loved best. Each day she learnt something different. One day it would be traditional dances that had been done in the villages for as long as anyone remembered and another day, the sacred dance rituals of the Healing Temple. She learnt dances appropriate to the seasons and the great festivals of the year, and new dances composed by the teachers. Most exciting of all, she began to rehearse with the rest of the Dancers for the great Midsummer Festival at the Temple.

One day Tama took the ten new Novices to the Temple to acquaint them with the place before the festival. She showed them the courtyard where they would be dancing, then took them into the Temple itself. A young Priestess greeted them, and sprinkled sacred water over their heads before she led them to the main altar.

They all stared, bewitched. On the altar stood a great stone, as tall as a man. As they approached the altar from the side, they'd seen the dull grey and green outside of it, but inside it was hollow and the hollow was full of glittering purple crystals. The Priestess put her hand into the space in the middle and invited the children to do the same. One by one they copied her, and came away looking astonished. Tiera, who went last, felt a tingling in her fingers that travelled right up her arm.

"This is the Great Geode," explained the priestess, "It is the largest amethyst ever seen in Kerran. It came from the mountains beyond the Sacred Forest and there are all sorts of stories about its magic powers. For example, they say that it could only be taken out of the mountain by supernatural powers, and that the cave where it was found was closed afterwards, so that nobody could ever enter it again. Then there's the legend of the guard-dog. If anybody tries to touch the Great Geode with evil intent, a terrifying black dog is supposed to appear. It's apparently as tall as a man, with huge fangs and eyes like fire!"

The children shivered deliciously. The boys especially loved scary stories.

"But it's not true of course!" laughed the Priestess. "The stories about the Geode's healing powers are true, though. There are many, many instances of people being healed by the Geode when nothing else had helped them. People come from all over Kerran to seek its healing power, especially at the Midsummer Festival - but you'll all be here to see that for yourselves before long, won't you?

CHAPTER FIVE

Tiera could not sleep. Tomorrow would be Midsummer Day and for the very first time she would be taking part officially in a major ceremony. It did not matter that on this day every single Dancer, even the tiniest, would take part. She would be among them, she would be part of the biggest ceremony of the whole year.

It would have been surprising if she could sleep on this, the shortest night of the year even without the prospect of tomorrow's festival. Earlier in the evening they had danced in the forest clearing, and she had seen the silver haired lady and her leaf-clad partner again shimmering in and out among the human dancers.

In bed now, she could hear rustlings and whisperings all around - she was not the only one who could not sleep! Even those who had danced in the Midsummer festival before were restless and excited. It was a relief when Cassie came to wake them well before dawn, for they must be at the Temple before the sun rose. As they tumbled out of bed and headed for the baths, the whispering turned to excited gossip. Who would be chosen to head the procession and carry the offerings? Who would have the privilege of pouring the libations?

"None of us!" said Selma, "We're too young. They'll be chosen from the Acolytes in the senior classes."

All the same, everybody had their favourites among the seniors, and here and there arguments broke out about which of them most deserved the honour. The same speculations were rife in the refectory where the entire community of Dancers shared a simple breakfast. It was too early to eat much, but Cassie insisted that everybody take something, for they had a long day ahead of them, and it would be hours before the general feasting began.

As soon as the untimely meal was over, Tiera and Selma raced to the dorter where they knew that fresh white robes would be waiting for them. Then it was back to the refectory where Muria would give them their final instructions. Gradually the hubbub subsided to an expectant hush as the First Dancer appeared on the platform with Ruid, Allya and Tama close behind her.

Tiera had never seen the quartet looking so radiant: all of them in white silk girded with gold sashes and wearing golden sandals. Ruid wore a silken tunic and a coronet of gilded leaves while the three women had fluid robes and garlands of flowers on their heads.

"Greetings, my dear ones on this Midsummer morning," said Muria. "I know that most of you have taken part in this festival before, but for those who have not, and anybody with a short memory....," she paused knowing that would provoke laughter, then smiled and went on: "let me quickly run through what will happen today. First, we will divide into four groups. All the boys are to follow Ruid, the junior girls will go with Allya, the senior girls with Tama and everybody else is to come with me. At the main door Cassie and her assistants will be waiting with the day students, and as soon as everybody is assembled, we will walk quietly..." she paused again and repeated "*quietly!* to the Temple. The rest you should all know by now as you have rehearsed it often enough. We will perform the opening dance, then the offerings and libation will be made."

Now the hall was utterly silent and still as everybody waited, breath held, to hear the names of the Dancers chosen for these duties. Muria went on:

"The offering of fruit is to be made by Ferna." A murmur ran round the hall as people welcomed or regretted the choice. Muria held up her hand for silence and continued:

"The offering of incense will be made by Paphi, the libation is to be poured by Nerron and finally, the offering of flowers is to be made by Tiera."

Tiera turned white and her knees nearly buckled as chaos broke out around her. Selma hugged her, Bron slapped her back, while elsewhere senior students grumbled at being passed over for a mere Novice. Behind her, Tiera heard Crissa whispering, "Not fair, not fair. Teachers' pet. Well, just you wait. I shall get even one of these days."

Once again, Muria held up her hand for silence.

"Yes, I know that Tiera is the newest of us all, but the choice is mine, as you all know and I have chosen Tiera because in the past three months she has worked harder than any student I have ever known. So now, please assemble in your groups and wait by the main door until I give the signal."

Bron made off to join Ruid and the rest of the boys while Tiera and Selma moved towards the group gathering round Allya but she bent and whispered in Tiera's ear, pointing to the group following Tama. Tiera nodded, nervously. The three older students who were to make offerings were all standing by Tama, and she was to join them.

The youngest girls with Allya set off first on the path to the Temple, followed by Ruid and the boys. Then Tama's group with Ferna, Paphi, Nerron and Tiera in the middle and finally came Muria and the other adult Dancers. At the Temple a guardian was waiting to open the picket gate to them and lock it again when the last Dancer had passed through. The main gates were still closed for it was not yet time for the people to be allowed into the compound. In fact,

Tiera marvelled, it was still not quite light, despite all that had already taken place that morning.

As they filed through the gate, a crowd of women and girls from Herbalists' Hall came forward to meet them, carrying great armfuls of flowers. These, Tiera discovered, were for the dancers' hair, and one by one they stepped forwards for the herbalists to garland them. The tiniest were each handed a basket filled with flower petals which they were to scatter on the ground.

Tama handed the basket of fruit to Ferna, a golden incense burner to Paphi, the flagon of wine to Nerron and a garland of flowers to Tiera.

"Now, you know what to do, don't you? When the opening dance is over, you are to walk slowly to the altar, kneel, and place your offering in front of the crystal. Ferna first, then Paphi, Tiera and Nerron, in that order. Nerron, you pour the wine onto the altar then put the flagon next to the flowers. Then turn and walk slowly back to me. I think that's clear?"

The four of them nodded. It was clear, even to Tiera, whose mouth was dry and heart thudding as she took her place among the other Dancers.

Now the Temple Guardians were opening the huge doors to reveal the great crystal while others threw back the main gates to the compound and townspeople began to flood in. For all that they were coming in their thousands, everything was quiet and orderly as people assembled round three sides of the great square, leaving space in the centre for the rituals that were enacted on this day every year. Then even the quiet murmur stopped and silence enveloped the multitude.

Now, a trumpet sounded from the roof of the temple as the first rays of the Midsummer Sun shone straight into the heart of the Great Geode. Tiera gasped, dazzled by the fiery reflections glancing off the myriad crystal points. A huge roar went up from the crowd as they greeted the dawn of the longest day, but nobody moved until the Sun's rays had moved on, leaving the crystal more gently glowing.

Now it was time for the Dawn Dance. First the tiniest girls skipped lightly here and there, scattering petals as they went, until their music drew to a close and they ran to kneel in two groups either side of the altar. Next came the boys' dance. They stamped and leapt over the flower-strewn ground, releasing all kinds of wonderful fragrances into the air. Dance followed dance, the junior girls spinning and swirling between the boys who were now kneeling on the sandy floor, then the senior girls performing a slow and solemn dance with formal arm movements. Muria led the adult Dancers in an undulating sequence in front of the altar, as she had done for so many years now.

Finally, it was time for the offerings. All the dancers, save the four chosen ones, had moved into two lines, creating a pathway between them that led to the altar. Tiera stood with Ferna, Paphi and Nerron near the main gates and waited for the music. Now that the moment had come, she felt utterly calm. The drums sounded, then the flutes and Ferna stepped forward at the signal, holding her basket of fruit high above her head. When she was half-way to the altar, Paphi moved forward holding the incense-burner before her.

As Ferna knelt to make the first offering, Tiera straightened her back, lifted her chin and began her walk to the altar. Like Ferna, she held her offering of flowers above her head. She felt thousands of eyes upon her and smiled a secret little smile as she thought how much her life had changed in so short a time, but she remained perfectly in time with the music. In the corner of her eye she could see Tama waiting at the head of the left-hand line of Dancers. She knelt and placed her flowers in front of the great amethyst, then rose gracefully and walked towards Tama as Nerron approached with his wine-jar.

Then it was over. The Dancers' dawn ritual completed, they gathered at the side of the Temple grounds to watch the other ceremonies. The crystal healers in their purple robes carried every kind of stone to the altar, where the High Priestess poured sacred water over them. The herbal healers, all dressed in green, brought baskets of flowers and leaves, phials of precious oils and jars of unguents to be blessed.

Once all the ceremonies were completed, it was time for any townspeople who wished to ask for healing or a simple blessing to come to the altar. Some drifted away after the rituals, but it was soon clear that many wished to be blessed on this special day, although the Temple was open for healing every day of the year, and a long queue snaked round the compound. Some of the most senior Dancers stayed behind, ready to work a healing if they were needed, but all the young people headed back towards the Dancers' Hall.

"I'm ravenous!" said Selma to Tiera, who had rejoined her friends, "I can't remember when I was last so hungry."

"Me too!" replied Tiera, though she could remember only too well the many times when her belly had ached from being empty.

Delicious aromas reached them even before they were indoors and they would have made a beeline for the dining-hall if Minna had not shooed them all upstairs to change and hang up their white robes, for they would be needed again in the evening. When they finally reached the hall, steaming bowls of soup were already on the tables and they fell to with gusto. Lunch went on for a long time, dish following dish, which was unusual in the House of Dance. Normally, the mid-day meal was a light one because there would be dance classes after it, but today was different; it was many hours since their pre-dawn breakfast and they would not be dancing again until after a light supper in the evening.

When they had finally finished eating, everybody was sent to lie down. Even if they did not sleep, they were expected to rest for several hours before they went back to the Temple to take part in the closing ceremonies. For a while, the girls talked quietly, but gradually the dorter grew quiet as, one by one, they drifted into sleep. Tiera thought she would no more be able to sleep than she had been during the night, so she was surprised when Minna bent over her almost five hours later, gently urging her to wake up and get dressed in her robe.

The evening ceremony was quite different, and less formal than that in the morning. After a chant of thanksgiving offered by the priestesses, everybody present formed circles ready for the closing dance. In the centre was the circle of priestesses. Around them stood the crystal healers and the astrologers, for the latter were too few to make a circle of their own, and beyond them came the herbalists. The dancers, who were the most numerous of the Temple servers, made a

71

circle beyond them, and finally several circles of such townsfolk as wished to join in - and they were many. As the music began, all the circles began to move in unison, a few steps to the left, then to the right but gradually the music got faster, and the rings swung more wildly from side to side until all the dancers were breathless, even those whose daily work was dancing. Abruptly the music ended, and laughing people dispersed in all directions. The Temple servers began to move towards their own halls and townspeople drifted in twos and threes towards the gates.

The four young Dancers who had presented the offerings were among the last to leave as one of the priestesses wished to thank them for their part in the ceremony. All the others had already passed through the picket gate and were climbing the path towards the hall when a rough hand was clamped over Tiera's mouth. She felt herself lifted off the ground and bundled inside some kind of coarse cloth. Ferna and Paphi, jostled aside by the kidnapper, began to scream.

"It's Tiera!" the girls cried, "Somebody has snatched her." Even as they called out, they were running towards the gate, for they were sure that was where any abductor would be taking her. Nerron followed, elbowing his way through the crowd, shouting Tiera's name. Tama, temple guardians and priestesses ran after them and pushed their way into the street, but there the crush was so dense there was no way of knowing in which direction she might have been carried.

"A girl in a white robe." "One of the Dancers." "Has anybody seen her?" "Fair hair, a robe like mine." They did not know then that Tiera had been pushed into a sack.

Somebody had seen a man carrying what might have been a child and hurrying that way. Somebody else thought they had gone in the opposite direction. Yet another swore there had been two men with a girl between them. The only thing that was certain was that there was no hope of finding anybody in such a throng.

Eventually Tama said, "I think the best thing we can do is get home as fast as possible and tell Muria what's happened. Nerron, run. We'll follow." The others nodded. They could think of nothing else. Nerron raced towards the picket gate. The girls stumbled, sobbing, after them.

In the confusion, nobody noticed four men creep into the shadows behind the altar.

CHAPTER SIX

It was a dismal group that gathered in Muria's study. The four most senior Dancers were there, that was to be expected. Ferna, Paphi and Nerron were huddled on cushions, shivering despite the rugs wrapped over their robes.

"I blame myself," said Tama, biting back tears, "I should have kept a closer watch. I was talking to one of the priestesses."

"No," said Muria, "that was a perfectly proper thing to do. The blame must rest with me. I should not have exposed the child by having her present an offering." Muria seldom showed her emotions, though nobody doubted that she felt them keenly, but now she, too, was weeping. Her whole body, usually so upright and poised, was crumpled and she looked very small.

"There is nothing to be gained from blaming ourselves," said Ruid gently, "Let's consider what's to be done next."

Muria dashed tears from her eyes and nodded.

"Yes, you are right Ruid."

They sat in silence for a few minutes, then Ruid spoke again.

"I think that, first thing in the morning, we must go to the city Vigiles..."

"Let's not wait until morning," Allya broke in, "the Vigiles are on duty day and night and by morning whoever has done this could have gone a long way."

"True. I'll go at once," said Ruid, already standing up.

"Can we come with you?" asked Ferna, "We were next to Tiera when it happened."

Ruid shook his head, smiling at her.

"I'm sure the Vigiles will want you to tell them exactly what happened, but I think not tonight. For now I will report that a child has been abducted and give them her description. The best thing you youngsters can do right now is have a hot drink and go to bed."

As if on cue, Cassie appeared in the doorway with a tray of mugs. Ruid, passing her on his way out, declined her offer of a drink and ran.

"Come in, Cassie," said Muria, "Come and join us

for a few minutes."

Cassie handed round fragrant mugs of camomile tea laced with honey, too, to calm the nerves.

"Well, I'll drink Ruid's mugful, then," she said as she sat down, "then I'd better see these young folk off to bed."

There was silence while everybody sipped the comforting liquid, then Cassie stood up and signalled the tearful young Dancers to do the same. As they made to leave, Muria said,

"You won't talk about this to anybody else, will you? Not until I have made an official announcement. I know you are old enough to trust."

They nodded solemnly, then Cassie ushered them off towards their dorters. Left alone, Muria, Tama and Allya still did not feel able to sleep.

"I can't understand why anybody would do such a thing," said Allya.

"Unfortunately, I can," said Muria, her face grim. "Remember what Tiera told us when we first found her? How her father was on the point of selling her. By running away she lost him a substantial sum of money.

77

If he saw her at the Temple it could have seemed like a perfect opportunity to get that money after all."

"How shall we break the news to the other children?" asked Tama, changing the subject.

"Well," said Muria thoughtfully, "Clearly we must tell the girls in her dorter and the ones she shares classes with. For the time being I think we should say nothing to the others. It's fortunate that there are no classes tomorrow. The day pupils will be at home with their families, and the others will go to the forest for the Midsummer picnic. The absence of one girl is less likely to be noticed than on a normal day and perhaps we will have some more encouraging news by the time they are back in their classes."

Privately, she thought this unlikely, but she did not want to discourage the younger teachers any more at this point.

At last, too tired to think any more, they exchanged comforting hugs and went their separate ways to bed.

Morning came all too soon, and the difficult task of breaking bad news. Allya and Tama were to talk to the class groups. Muria would go early to Tiera's dorter, taking Cassie with her to look after any girl who seemed particularly distressed. Ruid had already reported on his midnight visit to the Vigiles; they had sent men to search the slums near the river where Ruid thought Tiera had come from and, as expected, they wanted to talk to any dancer who was still in the Temple compound when Tiera was abducted.

Muria sat on the end of Selma's bed and gathered the other girls round her.

"Ruid has already spoken to the captain of Vigiles, and they are doing everything possible to find Tiera and bring her back to us. By tomorrow, we may well have some news but today is the day of the Midsummer picnic, and I do not want to spoil it for the rest of the school, so I trust you to keep this to yourselves for now." She was thankful that Cassie was with her, for she knew that Selma had been Tiera's closest friend since that very first day in the forest and was not surprised that she broke down when she heard the news. Emmi and Breda were very distressed, too, and Cassie decided to take the three of them back with her to the Sanctuary.

"Come on, my chicks, let's find you a nice hot drink and something a bit special for breakfast." She thought privately that Selma might need more than that to calm her, but a hot drink was always the first item on Cassie's agenda.

"Do we have to go to the picnic?" asked Jekka, "I won't feel much like playing games today."

"Nor me," said Ambla.

"Me neither," agreed Winna.

"Of course, my dears, I understand. Let me think what you might do instead. I will send somebody to tell you after breakfast."

Breakfast was a strange affair: the refectory seethed with excited young people looking forward to a day out while here and there clustered serious-looking groups, not speaking, barely eating. Each, for their different reasons, was glad when the meal was over. Tiera's dorter companions hovered by the door, not knowing where they should go next until Nessa came looking for them.

"Muria and Cassie have put their heads together and decided you should have your own private picnic."

"Oh!" The girls were not overjoyed at this news, but Nessa went on,

"Muria says you can bring books, sketching things, sewing, whatever you like. I'm coming with you and we'll have lunch in a different part of the forest, right away from the all the others. Meet me back here when you've collected whatever you'd like to bring with you and we'll set out as soon as Ruid gets back from the Vigiles with the people who saw what happened yesterday."

The day passed without any news. The dancers who had gone with Ruid to the Vigiles talked among themselves, Tiera's classmates and dorter companions did the same and when everybody else came back from the picnic, Muria sensed that trying to contain the bad news any longer was useless. Accordingly, when supper had ended she called for silence in the refectory.

"I'm afraid I have bad news to give you. One of our number is missing. We think she has been kidnapped. Now, I don't think there is any threat to anybody else, but for the time being none of you are to go beyond the grounds of the Hall without an escort from the Vigiles, and within the grounds themselves I want you to keep in twos and stay within sight of the main house."

In the shocked silence that followed, Henga from the senior class, raised her hand and asked,

"Please, who is missing?"

"It is Tiera."

A ripple of shock ran round the hall. In the short time that Tiera had lived in the Dancers' Hall most of the dancers had come to respect her, if not love her. Little groups of students whispered together, speculating on how and why she'd disappeared, wishing for her safe return, worrying about their own safety despite Muria's reassurances. But Allya, passing by one table on her way out, thought she heard Crissa whisper "Good riddance!"

"Something will have to be done about that girl," she thought but for now there were far more urgent things to think about.

Three more days went by, and there was still no news of Tiera. Somehow, the teachers ensured that lessons and rehearsals continued as usual, despite the tension that was palpable in every classroom. In particular, the adult dancers and some of the students needed to rehearse dances for a handfasting ceremony in two days' time. Nobody's heart was really in it, but they went through their steps meticulously and hoped they would have heard something encouraging before they had to perform them in public.

The morning of the ceremony arrived without any fresh developments, but those chosen to perform set off in procession to the Nuptial Temple. An equal number of men and women, boys and girls, they had an escort of Vigiles, for the captain had insisted that no children leave the grounds of Dancers' Hall without their protection. At the Temple they greeted the bridal pair with a flower dance, watched while the handfasting took place, then led the party out with a traditional festive dance. Somehow they managed to give an impression of joy that none of them felt.

They were leaving the temple when Bron noticed another wedding party approaching. He gripped Nerron's arm and hissed.

"Look! It's Tiera. I'm sure of it." He pointed at the bride; even though she was shrouded in veils they could see enough of her face and her distinctive hair to be almost certain it was their friend.

He hurtled down the temple steps shouting Tiera's name with Nerron close on his heels.

The two men on either side of the bride seized her arms and began to run.

"Follow them, follow them!" screamed Bron, running after them.

The Vigiles who were waiting to escort the dancers home took in the situation and gave chase, too.

The escaping men ran surprisingly fast despite the fact that they were half-carrying the girl between them, but Bron and Nerron were young and very, very fit and reached them in seconds. One of the men let go of Tiera's arm and swung a punch at Bron's chin, knocking him backwards. He rocketed into Nerron and both boys fell in a heap. But now the Vigiles had reached them. Two of them pulled the men away from the young girl, another caught her as she looked about to faint.

Now dancers were all round them, Tama was pulling the veil from the girl's face.

"Tiera! It really is you. Oh, thank heavens you are safe," she cried, gathering her in her arms. Tiera, sobbing, clung to her, but pandemonium had broken out around them. The Vigiles were having difficulty restraining the two men, for all that there were four of them, and that both men were old enough to be their fathers. They kicked and spat, twisted and bucked, but it was useless. The young law-keepers finally managed to twist chains round their arms and fasten them.

"Give me back my daughter!" bawled one man.

"That's my bride. I've paid good money for her," howled the other, "You lot have caused enough trouble already."

"Thieves!" "Kidnappers!" "The law is on my side, just you wait and see!"

The rest of the wedding party had caught up with them by now, two sobbing children among them. Tiera, without letting go of Tama, called out to them, and they ran to her, clinging to her clothes and saying her name over and over again.

"My brother and sister," Tiera explained.

The Vigile in charge of the escort drew Tiera gently

away from Tama and crouched down so that his face was level with hers.

"Do you know either of these men?" he asked.

She nodded dumbly.

"And is one of them your father?

Tiera nodded again. The man stood up and addressed Tama.

"We seems to have a rather complex situation here," he said, "This man claims to be the little girl's father and she agrees that he is. We may have to let her go with him."

"No! No!" shrieked Tiera.

The Vigile bent down again.

"Why don't you want to go with your papa?"

"He beat me. He was going to sell me. That man, he's called Fallod, gave him a lot of money so he could marry me."

"And how old are you?"

"I'm twelve, why?"

"That's too young to be married."

Tiera nodded. "That's why I ran away," she said.

Standing up once more, the Vigile spoke to Tama

again.

"This is far too complicated to settle here in the street. The father may well have a legal claim to the little girl, although she's clearly afraid of him. He could challenge your right to keep her. I'm afraid we'll have to take all of them to the Vigiles' post and see what the Captain has to say."

Tama nodded. The Vigile was right, however much she hated to admit it.

"I need to get my party back home," she said, "and I must report what has happened to Muria, our First Dancer."

The Vigile rubbed his chin thoughtfully. After a moment he said,

"Well, as the little girl's been found, and we've got these two ruffians under control, I suppose I can let you go without an escort. But the little girl will have to come with me and so will the two lads. They're witnesses as well as having been assaulted."

Tiera clung to Tama and shook her head.

"Don't be afraid," Tama said, gently detaching herself from Tiera, "Go with the Vigile now. I promise we'll get this sorted out as fast as possible, and nobody will make you do anything you don't want to."

CHAPTER SEVEN

Two groups faced each other in the office of the Captain of Vigiles.

On one side stood Tiera, Bron and Nerron. On the other stood Tiera's father and the man called Fallod, each still chained to two Vigiles.

Between them the Captain sat at a vast desk. Tiera's brother and sister were sitting at the back of the room with two kindly-looking women in Vigiles' uniform. The Captain spoke:

"This is beyond my jurisdiction. These two have assaulted the young lad as well as my officers. That much is clear and if that was all I could have dealt with it myself, but it looks as if they may have broken the laws regarding under-age marriage and heavens-knows what else as well. As for who might have a legal claim to the child - it's beyond me. It's possible the Dancers have contravened a few laws as well, sheltering a runaway for starters. I have no option but to refer the case to the Judiciars." He looked at a timekeeper on his desk and continued,

"There may still be time to seek a judgement today. That is, unless the court is very busy, but let's hope it's not. Lannon, go and arrange a couple of extra men to go with the prisoners and their guards. Oh, and send a messenger to Dancers' Hall - tell their chief and anybody else who might know anything to get down to the Judiciar's Hall as quickly as possible."

"Yes sir. What about the girl sir?"

The Captain looked at Tiera and sighed.

"I'll escort her myself, since she seems to be at the centre of all the trouble. The Vigilas can take care of the younger children," he said.

It was not far from the Vigiles' post to the Judiciars' Hall. The Vigile Lannon spoke to the guards at the gate then led the party up the steps. Hral and Fallod were still struggling and swearing but their guards hauled them up the steps ignoring their protests. At the top of the steps, Lannon spoke to another guard then turned to the Captain who followed close behind him and said,

"We're in luck, sir. There are not many petitioners today and one or other of the Judiciars should be able to hear us within the hour. "

The whole party was ushered into a side room where a scribe noted down everybody's names and the matters that the Judiciars were asked to pass judgement upon, then called a guard to take the party into the waiting room.

They followed him into a large room where the benches that ran all round the walls were full of people. The guards pointed to the benches nearest the door and indicated to the Captain of Vigiles that he should wait there with his party until they were called. The Captain had done this so many times before he sat with his eyes half-closed, but Tiera watched the door anxiously, praying that Tama or Ruid, in fact anybody from Dancers' Hall would arrive soon. Bron put his arm round her and tried to reassure her that their teachers would surely come at once when they got the Captain's message, and indeed it was not long before they arrived, breathless - all of them! Muria, Ruid, Allya and Tama rushed in, bringing Selma, Ferna, and Paphi with them.

After a while a guard came to call the Captain and

his party into one of the courtrooms. The Judiciar, dressed in a scarlet gown, sat on a raised dais at the far end. He looked with some surprise at the number of people involved in the case, then turned his attention to the papers the guard had handed him. Eventually he spoke:

"Well, well! Where shall we begin? H'mm, I think we should begin with the young lady at the heart of all the trouble."

The Captain took Tiera's hand and guided her to the centre of the platform. The Judiciar leaned towards her and said, very gently,

"Your name is Tiera, I think? Yes. Now Tiera, I want you to tell me in your own words what brings you here today," he looked at the paper in his hand again and went on, "You ran away from home?"

Tiera nodded nervously. She was afraid she would be in disgrace for doing that.

"Very well, let's start from there. Tell me why you ran away and everything that has happened since then."

"Sir, it was because my father wanted me to marry Fallod and I was frightened. I don't really want to be married to anybody, well, not until I'm a lot older, but I specially didn't want to marry Fallod, he's older than my father and he's fat and ugly."

At this there were angry mutterings from where Fallod stood between his guards.

"Silence!" said the Judiciar, "Go on please, Tiera. You ran away. What happened next?"

"I hid in the forest, and that's how I found the Dancers and they looked after me."

"And when was that?"

"In the Springtime, sir."

"Thank you, Tiera," the Judiciar consulted his paper again. "First Dancer Muria, can you confirm this?"

"Yes, sir. We were finishing our Spring Rites when Tiera fainted and fell out of a tree where she'd been hiding. She was emaciated, malnourished and covered in bruises, most of which were old ones. That it to say, they had not been caused by her fall. When she was sufficiently recovered to tell us her story she told us what she has just told you about the threat of a forced marriage, also that her mother died four years ago and since then her father had beaten her regularly. We believed her. The story was consistent with her physical state."

"And am I right in thinking that the Dancers have the ability to read thoughts?"

"Some us have, sir, but we only use it in certain circumstances."

"And would those circumstances include finding a stray child who has just fallen out of a tree? In other words, did you attempt to confirm her story in that way?"

"Yes sir, we did. We knew that she spoke nothing but truth."

"Thank you, First Dancer. Now, who else was present on that occasion?"

One by one, Bron and Selma, Ruid, Allya and Tama told how they had found Tiera in the forest, how they had examined her and taken her back to their Hall for healing. From time to time the Judiciar wrote down notes. He consulted the papers on his desk and said,

"Now, Tiera, you had better tell us how you came to be with your father and Citizen Fallod this morning."

Tiera described what had happened at the Temple

on Midsummer's Day then Tama, Ferna, Paphi and Nerron added their accounts.

"I see," said the Judiciar, "Unfortunately there does not seem to be any clear evidence as to how many people were involved, nor as to their identity, but we do know that Tiera was found with Citizens Hral and Fallod today. Four Vigiles as well as several Dancers attest to that." He paused, then went on:

"I think we should hear from Citizens Hral and Fallod now. Fallod first, please."

Fallod shuffled forward, still chained to two Vigiles.

"Citizen Fallod, it is alleged that you paid money to Citizen Hral in exchange for his daughter. Is this true?"

"Well, not exactly sir. The money was to pay for the wedding feast and the bride's clothing."

"Yes, that's what they all say!" said the Judiciar, wearily, "Were you not aware of the law forbidding the payment of bride-price?"

Fallod mumbled, looking increasingly uncomfortable.

"Do you know how old this child is," the Judiciar asked next.

"Yes sir, she's fourteen."

"I'm not! I'm twelve!" Tiera burst out.

"Hush! You'll have another turn to speak later," said the Judiciar, "You heard that, Citizen Fallod?"

"That's not what her father said, he told me she was fourteen," grumbled Fallod.

"I think we should hear Citizen Hral," said the Judiciar, and there was a pause while the Vigiles lugged Fallod back to one side and pushed Hral into his place.

"Citizen Hral, this girl is your daughter?"

"Yes sir."

"And you accepted money from Citizen Fallod for her?"

"The money was for the feast and wedding garments. You heard what Citizen Fallod said, sir."

"It was clearly well spent!" said the Judiciar, surveying Hral's elegant ensemble, the wedding robes that Tiera was still wearing, and glancing to where the younger children were sitting, all in fine clothes. "Unfortunately, that excuse has been used too often. The Courts have ruled more than once that such a payment is no different from a bride-price. Let us move on to the matter of Tiera's age. Citizen Fallod tells us that she is fourteen, but we have heard her deny that. I imagine you have her naming-scroll with you which would prove it?"

"Er, no, sir."

"Indeed? And you were on your way to her handfasting? Surely you knew you would have to present it to the priest?"

"It's lost, sir. Been lost a long time. In fact I'm not sure I've ever seen it, sir. I suppose my wife brought it with her when I married her, but I haven't seen it since she died."

Everybody gasped. Tiera, all the Dancers, Fallod, even the Judiciar.

"Are you saying that this child was born before you married her mother?"

"Yes sir," Hral said in a very small voice.

"So you are not her father?"

If Hral said anything at all, it was lost in a clamour of voices and it was several minutes before the Judiciar could restore order. Banging his desk, he shouted for silence.

"This completely changes the situation," he pronounced at last. "It is clear that Citizens Hral and Fallod have acted dishonestly, but far from clear who should have custody of the child. She must remain in the care of the Vigiles until that has been decided, but her case is so unusual I think it will have to be referred to the very highest authority, to Lord Therron himself."

At this, there were gasps from all sides. Lord Therron was the supreme ruler of Kerran. But the Judiciar was continuing,

"Captain, you will lock up these two men for the time being - they are clearly guilty of assault if nothing else - and arrange accommodation for the girl, and all parties are to present themselves at Lord Therron's court tomorrow at ten hours."

It was a bewildered party of Dancers who made their way back to the Hall, relieved that Tiera had been found safe and well, disappointed that they were not triumphantly taking her home with them, and - the grown-ups at least - worried about the outcome of tomorrow's hearing.

Lord Therron's palace was one of the finest buildings in Allegria, second only to the Temple of Healing in size and beauty. A line of guards in fine uniforms stood in the courtyard, behind them a great flight of steps led up to a noble portico.

Tiera arrived in the square before the palace with Dilla and Frol and the two Vigilas who had cared for them overnight and gazed at the building in awe. She had passed by here once or twice but had never imagined she would ever go inside, still less that when she did, it would be to decide her whole future.

Before long, the Captain of Vigiles arrived with his prisoners and their guards, and almost at the same time, from the opposite direction, came the group of dancers. As before, the Captain spoke to a guard and they were led up the great steps, handed over to another guard and shown into an antechamber. A black-gowned scribe followed them, and spent some time talking to the

Captain, shaking his head from time to time, nodding at others and writing notes. As he left, he turned to Tiera and said,

"Well, young lady, you should feel honoured that Lord Therron himself is to give judgement in your case."

Tiera was not at all sure that she wanted to be so honoured. She just wanted it all to be over and to be back at Dancers' Hall. But now yet another guard, in a different kind of uniform, was coming to fetch them to the Lord Therron's audience chamber. Tiera looked around the huge hall, at its high gilded ceilings and the great widows running down each side decorated with scenes from the history of Kerran and its heroes.

At the far end of the hall was a raised dais and there the man who was clearly Lord Therron sat on a gold throne. He was wearing a purple gown embroidered in gold, and he had a slim circlet of gold around his silver hair. He was reading a thick pile of papers, but after a few minutes he looked up from his reading and asked for First Dancer Muria, Citizen Hral, Citizen Fallod and the child Tiera to step forward.

"I have considered this case at some length," he said, " In fact, I confess I have spent a sleepless night as a result of it! It is, indeed, a complicated business, but now that I have read all the notes, I am ready to pronounce judgement."

His voice was deep and rich, but he spoke surprisingly gently and there was a hint of humour in his eyes. All the same, Tiera felt sick for fear that she would not be allowed to go back to Dancers' Hall.

"I will deal first with Citizens Hral and Fallod," he continued. "Both of them have broken the law concerning the payment of bride-money, and under-age marriage. These are very serious offences and in the case of Citizen Hral, made worse by the fact that he is not related to the child in question. Our judgement is that Citizen Fallod is to be fined five thousand scudos."

There were gasps as the severity of the fine, but Lord Therron ignored them and went on.

"Citizen Hral is found guilty of accepting bride-money, lying about the age of the child concerned, lying about his relationship to her, and of cruelty to the child. I have no choice but to impose a prison sentence of seven years."

"My lord! Please don't send him to prison," cried Tiera, "there will be nobody to look after my brother and sister."

"I'm coming to that in a moment, my child, but I promise your siblings will be well cared for. Captain, take the two of them away."

Two Vigiles dragged Hral off while two more unfastened Fallod's chains, and escorted him away to pay his fine.

"Now, the matter of the children. I have thought long and hard about this and decided that Dilla and Frol are to be made wards of court, and placed in a loving foster-home. As for Tiera, she too is to be a ward of court, but I feel she is old enough to make her own choice about where she will live. Tiera, step forward please."

Nervously, Tiera came and stood in front of Lord Therron.

"Tiera, do you understand what "ward of court" means?"

"No my lord."

"It means that when a young person does not have any parents or a suitable person to look after them, the Judiciars can make decisions that would usually be made by a parent, such as where they should live and what schooling they are to have. I am going to appoint a Judiciar to be responsible for you in the future, but as I have just said, I think you are old enough to choose where you want to live. So, would you rather stay with your brother and sister, or return to Dancers' Hall?"

Tiera looked wildly around her: at Lord Therron, at Dilla and Frol, at her Dancer friends, at Lord Therron again. She put her head in her hands and began to cry.

"Tiera, if you want to be a Dancer, we will make sure that you can see your brother and sister whenever you want," said Lord Therron gently.

Tiera looked up, almost unbelieving. Slowly, a smile spread across her face.

"Then I would like to go back to Dancers' Hall!" she said.

At this, a cheer went up from the party of Dancers, and even Lord Therron did not try to silence them.

CHAPTER EIGHT

The Lady Khoda stormed up and down the great hall. Her silken skirts hissed like snakes as she turned, her heels struck sparks off the stone floor and echoed back from the stone walls and the vaulted ceiling. Her black hair billowed like a storm-cloud round her face, and her eyes flashed lightning. She came to a halt in front of the heavily-carved chair where Lord Yevon cowered and jabbed her forefinger at his face.

"Coward!" she hissed, "Lily-livered milksop. Spineless namby-pamby. Yellow-bellied poltroon. I want that crystal. You were within inches of it - so what stopped you grabbing it? A dog! My noble husband was afraid of a dog! Well, I can tell you one thing, my dear Yevon: unless I get that crystal you won't be my husband much longer. I shall be gone from here, I shall divorce you - oh, I can find plenty of reasons, I promise you."

"Be reasonable, my love," Lord Yevon stammered.

"Reasonable!" she retorted, "I've been reasonable

too long. I have wanted that crystal for years and you know it. I want the power that only a huge geode can bring. You promised to bring me that crystal on Midsummer Day and now it is a month later and still no crystal. You will get me that crystal, or else. And I don't care how. Just get it. That is....." she paused and lowered her voice, "Unless you can find me an even bigger, even more powerful crystal!" With which she swept away down the hall and up the spiral staircase to her chamber.

Lord Yevon mopped sweat from his forehead. His hand shook as he rang the bell for his steward. In fact, he shook all over, his chins quivering like jelly.

"Quar! Fetch me a drink of mel. I need one, my goodness, do I need one! Her ladyship is displeased."

"Yes m'lord," said Quar, who had heard every word from his niche behind the great purple curtains.

Lord Yevon sat reflecting on what his wife had said: that he was afraid of a dog! But it was no ordinary dog, and she knew that perfectly well. As tall as a man, and black as night, with eyes like red lanterns. One look at its fangs and he knew it would tear him to pieces if he took even one step nearer to the great crystal. Unlike the lady Khoda, he did not consider himself particularly cowardly but there was no way he would go within yards of that beast again although, he reflected, the Lady Khoda in her present mood was almost as terrifying! Cunning was what was needed, not more attempts to steal the great crystal from the Temple.

It had been a crazy idea anyway. He'd only undertaken it to please the Lady Khoda and even then he half-knew that four men would not be able to lift the great crystal, but they had never got near enough to try. The dog had made sure of that. He hadn't known about the dog. He would have to put his mind to ways of finding an even larger, even more splendid crystal.

When the steward came back, Lord Yevon said,

"Sit down, Quar. Pour yourself a drink, too." He'd noticed that the servant had already put two goblets on the tray!

Lord Yevon suspected that Quar eavesdropped on everything that went on in the hall and Quar knew that his master thought that, but it was never mentioned by either of them. As far as Lord Yevon was concerned, this was quite a useful arrangement. Quar was astute, he often made really useful suggestions and if he, Lord Yevon, did not need to explain a situation in much detail it saved a lot of time!

So, without any preamble he asked,

"Quar, if you wanted to buy a crystal, where would you go?"

"I'd go down to the harbour, m'lord. All the merchants have their businesses there: import and export, m'lord, cloth and grain and spices and..."

"Never mind all that. I'm only interested in crystals."

"You will find them there, too m'lord. Many fine stones come from overseas though the foreign traders are always keen to buy what comes out of our own mines."

"Our own mines? I never knew there were such things!"

"Oh yes, m'lord, Kerran is rich in minerals of all kinds, crystals among them."

"H'mm, food for thought. But I think I will see what the merchants have to offer first. Yes, we shall go to the harbour in the morning, Quar. Find me the plainest clothes I've got for the morning - I don't want to draw attention to myself.

"Yes, m'lord."

"Now, pour me another drink and then I shall go to bed."

****

The great harbour of Allegria was an impressive sight: ships from many lands stood at anchor, their sails furled: big ships, little ships with men scurrying up and down gangways with their loads. Lord Yevon wondered idly where they had come from and where they would sail to but would not tarry to find out. His business was with the traders in precious stones. He followed Quar past the rows of warehouses facing the wharf until they came to a street lined with shops. Ignoring the cloth merchants, the spice traders, the sellers of knives and swords, he stopped at a window that almost dazzled him with the light reflecting off quartz and emerald, amethyst and citrine.

"Wait there for me," he said to Quar as he ducked in at the low doorway. Inside he found himself surrounded by such an array of stones that it almost took his breath away. There were crystals as big as his fist and others so small and delicate they looked as if they would break if he touched them. There were rubies and agates, amethysts and chunks of lapis lazuli and countless stones whose names he did not know. Some were mounted on rings or pins, some were just as they had come out of the earth, some were on shelves, others in glass cases, and in the middle of the array sat an old man examining a diamond through a powerful magnifying glass.

The old man ignored him and went on scrutinising the stone. Lord Yevon was not used to being ignored. At the same time, he did not want to antagonise the merchant, so he cleared his throat loudly, and shuffled his feet to make his presence known. Eventually, the old man laid down his glass and looked up.

"What can I do for you sir?" he asked.

"I am looking for an large amethyst, a very large amethyst, in fact an extremely large amethyst."

The old man did not reply, but put his head through a small door at the back of the shop and said something Lord Yevon could not hear. After a moment, a young lad came through the door and took the old man's place behind the counter.

"Call me if anybody comes in," said the old man, and signalled Lord Yevon to follow him into the back room. He drew out a chair for Lord Yevon and sat down facing him.

"How big?"

"At least as big as the one in the Temple," Yevon replied.

"The Great Geode!" the old man said, then shook his head. "I don't deal in stones that size. Most of my wares are made into jewellery, or wands for the healers. Besides, you don't want a merchant, you need a miner. The Great Geode was found here in Kerran, though I doubt they'll ever find another like it."

Ignoring the latter remark, Yevon asked,

"Where can I find a miner? Do you know any?"

"Of course! I export as many stones as I buy in. I depend on the miners for half of my trade. But they don't all cut amethysts. In fact, good amethysts are getting harder and harder to find, especially large ones. I think Wilkin would be your best choice, in fact probably your only choice. His family have been mining crystals for generations."

"Where can I find him?"

In reply, the old man wrote the name of a place on a scrap of paper and sketched a rough map next to it.

"Here," he said, "Tell him I sent you. He doesn't talk to everybody."

They went back into the shop and Lord Yevon looked around him once again. Any other time he would have bought some exquisite jewel, or more than one, for the Lady Khoda, but he knew that now she would simply throw it back in his face. He had to find a giant amethyst. That or nothing. So he thanked the old man and left.

"Have you ever heard of a man named Wilkin?" he asked Quar, who was waiting for him outside.

"No m'lord."

Lord Yevon took the paper from his pocket and handed it to the steward.

"Well, do you know this place?"

Quar examined the paper and looked up, surprised.

"Yes, m'lord, of course, Lusa is on your own lands!"

"Where? where?"

"About eight leagues from Castle Yevon, m'lord, near the edge of the forest."

"Go and find this Wilkin for me. Take your horse and go straight away. I can ride home from here on my own. Find him, and bring him to me."

"Yes, m'lord," said Quar, amazed that his master did not know the name of a hamlet that he owned, that his father and grandfather and great-grandfathers before him had owned for as long as anybody could remember. Well, it shouldn't be difficult to find this man Wilkin: Lusa was a small place.

****

Towards noon the following day, Quar rode into the courtyard of Castle Yevon with Wilkin the miner following. Neither were in a good mood. Quar had found the cabin where Wilkin lived without any difficulty, but it was too late, too dark to set out for the castle by the time the man returned from his day's labours so Quar had spent the night on a lumpy pallet and broken his fast on lumpy porridge. Wilkin was no happier: he was missing a day's work but dared not refuse Lord Yevon's summons. Lord Yevon, after all, owned his cabin and the whole of Lusa and could easily turn him out if he disobeyed. Besides, he had ridden a borrowed horse for eight leagues, a very bony horse, and his bottom ached!

Dismounting extremely stiffly, he followed Quar through the great doors.

Quar shook a pageboy he found lolling among the suits of armour in the entrance hall and sent him running to the master.

"Tell Lord Yevon that Wilkin the miner is here, and hurry," he said.

Soon the boy came scurrying back and said the master would receive Wilkin immediately, and that Quar was to bring the man to Lord Yevon's private study.

In the study, Lord Yevon stepped forward and grasped Wilkin by both hands.

"Sit down, sit down my good man! Quar, bring us some chai, order food, have it sent up here."

Wilkin sat nervously on the edge of his chair. He was not used to such grandeur. Even in a small room such as his private study, Lord Yevon favoured heavy tapestries, carved wood and stained glass in the windows.

Lord Yevon studied him carefully: a small man, wiry and stooped, his silver hair was cut like a rough brush above his lined face. Dwarflike, Lord Yevon thought, well suited to crawling about in caves.

"You must be wondering why I've sent for you," Lord Yevon said at last.

"Yes, my lord," the man replied.

"You're a miner. I understand you mine amethysts? Is that correct?"

"Yes, my lord, my family have mined crystals for as long as anybody can remember. Five generations at least. Quartz and amethyst and citrine mostly, you usually find them together."

"Yes, yes," said Lord Yevon, impatiently "I am only interested in amethysts. Large amethysts. Where do you find them?"

"In the caves under your lands, my lord."

"Really? I had no idea there were caves here."

Wilkin gaped. He was as surprised that the Lord Yevon did not know about the caves, as Quar had been when he realised that his master did not know of the existence of Lusa.

"Yes, my lord, the caves have been mined for hundreds of years. It was a great industry in my great-grandfather's time, but we don't bring that much out these days. The biggest caves have been closed off for a hundred years or so and there's only myself and my son working a few small grottoes now."

"But you still find amethysts?"

"Yes, my lord."

"Very well, I want you to find me a large one, a very large one. At least as large as the one in the Temple."

"The Great Geode! That's impossible, my lord. It came from the Grand Chamber, that's the biggest and deepest of the caves. They say one of my ancestors found it, though it was so long ago nobody knows. Nobody has been into the Grand Chamber for a hundred years or more, not since the rock-fall that killed my great-grandfather and closed it off, and nobody has ever found a stone that size anywhere else. We're pleased if we find amethysts as big as our fingers these days."

"Nothing is impossible," said Lord Yevon. "These caves are below my lands, you say? So, I own them! I own your cabin. I own Lusa. If I tell you to find me a second Great Geode you will find it. I will provide all the money, all the men you might need. You will open up the Grand Chamber, and you will search for the biggest amethyst this land has ever seen. Have I made myself clear?"

"Yes, my lord," replied a very unhappy Wilkin.

CHAPTER NINE

After the dramas of Midsummer, life at Dancers' Hall gradually returned to normal, though it took time. When the triumphant party returned from Lord Therron's, Tiera was so radiant and the others so relieved that nobody thought about what she had been through in the past few days. Not Muria, not even Tiera herself. It was only when Selma reported to Cassie that Tiera had woken screaming from a nightmare, that anybody thought to arrange another healing dance for her.

Cassie had gone straight to Muria with Selma's news.

"Oh! Why on earth didn't I think about this before?" cried Muria.

"Why didn't *any* of us think about it?" said Cassie, "Well I guess it was because we were all so glad to see the poor chick safely back here, and she's been floating about on a cloud, at least when she was awake."

"We must work a healing for her straight away - I

think as soon as classes have finished this afternoon. Yes, I'll speak to the others, and to Tiera herself of course, and organise it."

Leaving the refectory after breakfast, Muria called Tiera to come with her.

"Tiera, I hear you had a really bad dream," she said, "do you feel like telling me what it was about?"

"I was suffocating. My fa..., I mean Hral, had pushed me into a sack and I couldn't breathe."

"That's what happened at the Temple, isn't it?"

"Well, I'm not sure who it was. They threw the sack over my head before I could see. But I imagine it was him."

"Tiera, I think we should make a healing dance for you today. For your mind especially, so that you don't have any more nightmares. Would you like that?"

"Oh yes! That would be so kind. Thank you."

"Then go to Cassie in the Sanctuary when you finish lessons this afternoon. And now you'd better run or you'll be late for your first dance class!"

****

Two weeks after Tiera's return, classes ended for the summer. Dinner that evening was a special feast; Cassie had produced all the most popular dishes, and there were wild strawberries from the forest with delicate ices to follow.

After dinner there was a scramble to finish last-minute packing, for most of the students would be going home to their families in the morning. Some of the adult dancers planned to go travelling, too, while those who were staying at the Hall looked forward to a month of relaxation. Only a handful of students would be staying in Hall, those who had no home to go to and a few whose homes were very distant. Of the teachers, only Muria would be there the whole time.

For Tiera, there was no question of going anywhere else: the Hall was now her home. Yssa and Lyria were staying behind, too, and Yssa's brother Milon, though Tiera did not know them well enough to know their circumstances. They were older than her and their paths seldom crossed in the daily routine of classes.

After the flurry of hugs and goodbyes the whole

place was strangely quiet. There were no classes to go to, nothing she absolutely had to do, so Tiera took a book and wandered into the garden. Now that she had mastered reading, it was one of her greatest pleasures, second only to dancing. She took a rug from the dorter and spread it near the trees at the furthest end of the gardens and lay down to enjoy her story. She was deep in the tale when she thought she heard a voice, but looked round and could see nobody. She went back to her book, but the voice came again. She put the book down and sat up.

"Who's there?"

"I'm here, look up."

She looked up, turning her head this way and that but could still see nobody, only a squirrel sitting on the branch of a beech tree overhead.

"Yes, I'm here, I need to talk to you," said the squirrel.

"I'm dreaming!" thought Tiera, but the squirrel was scrambling down the trunk of the tree and coming towards her.

"We need your help," said the squirrel, "there is

trouble in the Sacred Forest and we can't stop it by ourselves. We need humans to help."

"What is wrong?" asked Tiera. Already it felt perfectly normal to be talking with a small animal.

"Somebody is chopping down trees. Not one or two, here and there, but a great many all in the same place. We're losing our homes, and so are our friends the birds. The men who are doing this trample the plants underfoot, they drag the logs across the ground with chains. The plants are dying and the mice and voles and insects are losing their homes too."

"That is terrible!" cried Tiera, "What can I do to help you?"

"Go and tell somebody older than yourself, somebody who loves the forest. Please don't delay."

"I'll go and tell Muria. She loves the forest. She'll know what to do."

"Thank you," said the squirrel and disappeared among the trees.

Tiera scooped up her book and rug and ran as fast as she could in search of Muria. She did not have to look far, for Muria like herself was reading, on the lawn in front of her study. Tiera flung herself down on the ground beside her and panted,

"There are men cutting down lots of trees in the Sacred Forest. A squirrel told me to tell you."

Muria put down her book at once.

"This is serious," she said, "I think I should send a message to Lord Therron. And how long have the animals been talking to you?"

Tiera stared at her for a moment, then began to laugh. In her haste to find Muria she had completely forgotten that it was only a few minutes ago that she was surprised to hear a squirrel talking! But she saw that Muria was looking at her intently.

"Since just now," she said, "I was reading at the far end of the garden and I heard somebody talking to me, and it was a squirrel and that's what he told me."

Muria got to her feet and said,

"Come indoors with me. I'm going to find somebody to take a message to Lord Therron, and then I think you and I need to have a serious talk." Once inside her study, Muria went straight to her desk, took a quill and ink and said,

"Tiera, my dear, sit down and repeat as exactly as you can what the squirrel said to you," and she began to write as Tiera told her how men were damaging the forest, how the creatures were losing their homes. Muria wrote rapidly as she spoke, then blotted the scroll and sealed it.

"I'm going to find one of the boys to run to Lord Therron with this. Stay there, I should'nt be many minutes."

When she came back, she sat down facing Tiera and said,

"Tiera, ever since you arrived at Dancers' Hall, I have suspected that you had certain gifts, partly because of something that Bron and Selma said to me that very first day. Now I'm almost certain. It's not everyone who has serious conversations with the forest creatures, and the creatures do know who to come to when they need to talk. Tell me about your mother."

Tiera was puzzled by the change of subject. How did her mother connect with squirrels that talked? But she began to describe her:

"She was so gentle, and she had a lovely voice. She

would sing songs to us ever day."

"What did she look like?" asked Muria softly, "Was she petite? Was she fair like you?"

"No, she was very tall, and she had black hair and beautiful brown eyes."

"And you never knew your real father?"

"No, I always thought Hral was my father until the day in Lord Therron's court."

"Tiera, I think your father was a fairy. That means that you are a half-fay," she paused, "as I am."

Tiera stared at her teacher, lost for words.

"Yes, I know it is not easy to take in all at once. And it is never easy to feel that one is different from the people around you, but you are by no means alone here in Dancers' Hall. I suspect there are more of us here with one human and one fairy parent than anywhere else in Allegria, perhaps anywhere in Kerran."

"Who else?" whispered Tiera.

"Your first teacher, Liana, for one, then there are Lyria, the twins Yssa and Milon, and I suspect that young Arron may be one of us, too. That is 6 or 7 half-

125

fays in a community of about 60 Dancers, when you'd be fortunate to find one in five thousand in Kerran generally."

"Why?"

"I think it is partly because we feel more comfortable here than in society generally. We can use our special abilities without being made to feel that we are strange. And I am *sure* that half-fays are drawn here because the Dancers have a duty to protect the Sacred Forest. That's why our Hall was built where it is, between the forest and the Temple. The fairies are the original guardians of the forest, since long before humankind, and we work with them. So, it is natural that children with some fairy blood feel drawn to become Dancers, apart from the fact that fairies love to dance, better than almost anything."

At this, Tiera smiled and nodded.

"And the fact that the half-fays can see and talk with full fairies, as well as hear the animals, as you have learnt today, is very important. It means that if there is anything they need to tell humans, we can hear and pass it on."

Again, Tiera nodded, for that was exactly what had happened this morning. Muria put an arm round her shoulder and said,

"There is more you will learn, but I think that's enough for today. It's noon, and time we went to eat some of Cassie's good food, because we need to take care of these human bodies of ours."

As they walked across the lawn, Tiera asked shyly,

"What did Selma and Bron say that made you think I might be a half ... what is it? A half-fay?"

"Apparently you asked them the identity of the silver-haired lady dancing with us at the Spring Rites, and when Bron said it was me, you replied that you knew who Muria was, but this was somebody else, and that she was dancing with a man dressed in green leaves. I knew at once that you were either one of us, or you had the Sight, as some full humans have, because it could only have been the Lady Titania and the Green Lord. Have you seen them again since then?"

"Yes, I saw them on Midsummer's Eve, and a lot of others with them."

"That doesn't surprise me at all. Midsummer's Eve is one of the most magical nights of the whole year, especially in the forest."

The refectory had been closed for the summer break, and they ate in Cassie's kitchen, sitting round the scrubbed wooden table. Tiera looked with new eyes at her table companions, especially those who Muria had named as half fairy people. She noted that Lyria had very fair hair like herself, while Yssa and Milon both had red hair and freckles like the teacher Liana, and all three of them had deep green eyes. There was something else about them though, something akin to a family likeness. Yes, that was it. Sitting with them and Muria round this table, Tiera felt that she was part of a family. Muria often said that the whole community of Dancers was a family, and that was true in many ways, but it was too big to feel like a real family to Tiera. Sitting in Cassie's kitchen with these people she felt at home.

It made her think about her human family, though, and she determined to ask Muria if she could visit Dilla and Frol one day soon.

When the meal was finished, Muria spoke quietly to Lyria, Yssa and Milon and ushered the three of them, together with Tiera, outside to sit in the sun.

"I think it is time Tiera got to know the three of you better," she said, smiling, "This morning I told her what I have suspected for a long time, that she is one of us!"

None of the trio looked particularly surprised.

"I've wondered for quite a while," said Milon.

"I'm going to leave you together, I have work to do indoors. It would be nice if you'd talk to Tiera a bit about yourselves."

They sat down on the grass. Nobody quite knew where to start, and they were silent for a bit, then Tiera asked,

"Do the animals talk to you? Do you see fairy people?"

"Yes and yes," laughed Yssa, "And can you hear other people thinking?"

"No," said Tiera, "though I often have a pretty good idea!

"I think," said Milon quietly, "that if you practised a bit you'd find you could tell fairly accurately what most people were thinking. Probably not as well as Muria - she's been doing it for a very long time!"

"Right," said Lyria, "Practice starts now! I'm going to concentrate on something, and see if you can tell what I'm thinking." She looked straight at Tiera, and the others were quiet. After a few moments, Tiera said,

"You're thinking that you all know how I arrived at Dancers' Hall but I don't know how you did."

"Bravo!" said Lyria, "Try somebody else. Yssa, your turn."

"Yssa, you are wondering what we'll have for dinner tonight!"

"Correct! Now try Milon," said Yssa.

It took Tiera a moment or two longer to decipher Milon's thoughts, and when she did, she blushed.

"You were thinking about dinner, too, but you were also thinking Tiera is very pretty." She blushed even deeper.

Milon went rather red, too, but he laughed and said,

"We're going to have to mind what we think when you're around, I can see that! Though of course it is easier when we are helping you by concentrating."

Yssa, also laughing, said,

"It may be easier, but it's a very good way to start. The more of this you do, the easier it will be pick up thoughts that people aren't particularly directing at you."

"Thank you. I'll keep practising and I'd be really grateful if you'd help me sometimes, but can I ask you something?"

"Fire away!" said Yssa.

"Lyria was thinking that I didn't know how you all arrived at Dancers' Hall. Would it be rude to ask how you did?"

"My grandmother brought me here to beginners classes when I was seven because I screamed and kicked until she did!" replied Lyria.

"What about you?" asked Tiera, turning to Yssa.

"Milon and I were left at the gate in a basket when we were a few weeks old."

"What on earth did they do with you? I mean, there's nobody here who'd have time to take care of a baby, let alone two of them."

"Oh, Muria arranged for us to be fostered, enrolled

us in beginners classes when we were old enough, and moved us into the Hall when we were ten."

The mention of fostering reminded Tiera again of her brother and sister, and she determined to speak to Muria about them next time she saw her. But now the sun was going down and it was growing chill in the garden and the four new friends got up and moved towards the house.

"We'll play some more mind-games with you tomorrow" promised Lyria as they parted company.

CHAPTER TEN

The rest of the summer break was idyllic; the weather was perfect day after day and meals were eaten in the garden as often as not. In the second week Cassie left for a well-deserved rest at the home of her sister who lived by the sea, leaving the cooking to Minna and Nessa who were more than happy to serve cold, picnic-style buffets a good deal of the time.

As soon as Tiera asked about visiting her little brother and sister, Muria made arrangements for her to do so, and for Beatta, their foster-mother, to bring Dilla and Frol to visit Dancers' Hall as well. It made Tiera so happy to see them looking well-fed and contented and they enjoyed playing in the big gardens and being made a fuss of. Milon, in particular, played wonderfully inventive games with them.

The only shadow over this happy time was another message from the forest creatures about the destruction of the Sacred Forest. A few days before the end of the summer break Tiera was in the garden with Lyria, Yssa and Milon when a whole flock of birds arrived and told them that tree-cutting was still going on, but in a different part of the forest. They knew that Lord Therron had sent men to investigate the trouble after he got Muria's message, for he had sent a reply promptly, but now the pigeons and woodpeckers, the thrushes and tree-creepers were saying that the felling had simply been moved to a more remote area and that it was going on at an even faster pace than before.

The quartet went at once to Muria to report this new development. She listened to them with an increasingly long face.

"This is even worse than I imagined," she said, "Somebody is defying Lord Therron's authority, as well as destroying the forest. We must let Lord Therron know at once. Milon, if I write a message, would you take it to the palace as quickly as you can?"

"Yes, of course I will," replied Milon, and Muria sat down and wrote furiously.

It was not long before he was back with a message that Lord Therron wanted to talk to all the young Dancers who had received messages. Muria sent him to call the girls in from the garden, and set off with them to the palace. This time, instead of the great hall in which Tiera's future had been decided, they were shown into a small private room.

"Sit down, my dear young people and I will call for some refreshments for you, then I would like you to tell me exactly how this sorry business was brought to your attention."

They settled themselves on the richly brocaded divans piled with cushions, and while they waited for a servant to come back with a tray of cooling drinks, Muria began to introduce them by name.

"Lyria, Yssa, Milon, I am happy to make your acquaintance and young Tiera is of course an old friend!"

Tiera blushed with pleasure at being termed a friend of Kerran's overlord! Now she told him about how the squirrel had talked to her in the garden and he nodded seriously as she spoke.

"Yes, and as a result I sent two experienced foresters, with a party of guards accompanying them, to find out what was happening and stop it. They found the men who were cutting down trees and came back with assurances that they had no idea they were doing anything wrong and would stop felling at once. Now, who heard this new message?"

"All of us, my lord," said Milon, "We were all in the garden today when about twenty birds flew down, in a very agitated state and told us that trees were being cut down in a more distant part of the forest, and even faster than before."

"And you all heard this?"

"Yes, my lord," they said, all together.

"Then, am I right in supposing that you are all half-fay?"

"They are!" laughed Muria.

"Interesting, very interesting, but to return to the problem: I shall send a larger body of men this time, more guards especially, with my authority to arrest anybody found cutting trees or damaging the forest in any way. We must get to the bottom of this as soon as possible. I can hardly tell you how grateful I am to you all, Dancers, for your part in this."

"Lord Therron, it is part of our duty to care for the

forest, as you know, and those of us with fairy blood feel perhaps more responsible than any," said Muria.

"Then I give thanks that there is such a delightful group of you at Dancers' Hall and I promise that I will keep you in touch with everything that happens. Unless, that is, you find out before I do!" he smiled, "In which case I'm sure you will let me know."

****

Now it was nearly time for the Dancers' to reassemble and prepare for their Autumn activities. Ruid, Tama and Allya came back a few days before the students were due and spent many hours in Muria's study, planning for the next few months and deciding who would move up a class. Cassie got back about the same time and set about organising all the domestic arrangements. Then came the great influx as the students returned.

Tiera gave Selma a huge hug when she got back: she'd missed her despite making new friends while most of the students were away and they had masses to tell each other while Selma unpacked and settled herself back into the dorter. At dinner that evening there were more stories to be told of what each of them had done during the holiday.

Tiera found, though, that her new ability to read other people's thoughts was a problem now that the Hall was full again. She was distracted by random ideas from people around her all the time she was talking with her friends. She was on the point of telling Selma about her difficulty when she suddenly felt reticent about it. She was not sure how her friend would react, not sure whether half-fays were supposed to talk about such things to people without fairy blood. So she kept quiet and resolved to seek advice from Muria if she could or, as Muria was clearly going to be very busy at this point in the year, she thought she might ask one of her trio of new friends.

At the end of dinner, she spotted the three of them about to leave the refectory together, and made her way across to them.

"May I ask your advice about something?" she asked.

"Yes, of course," said Milon, putting an arm round her shoulders and ushering her out of the hall. They stood in the entrance hall and Milon asked,

"What's the trouble?"

"This business of hearing other people's minds. It was fine when there were just the four of us here, but now I can hear everybody when I'm trying to have a normal conversation with just one or two people."

"Ah! You have to learn how to be selective, how to shut out what you don't want to hear," Milon said, "Look, it's a bit late now, but I'll get the girls together after classes tomorrow and we'll show you how."

Classes did, indeed, start in earnest the following morning, and Tiera had no time to think about the problem between the first dance class of the season, a music lesson and double maths! But at lunch time it burst in on her again, as she struggled to talk normally with Grammi and Ambla while picking up a jumble of thoughts from everybody else at her table. She consoled herself with the knowledge that it was only a few hours until Milon and the older girls would teach her how to prevent that, and went off with a lighter heart to her afternoon dance class.

Ruid taught this class, to Tiera's surprise for she'd always thought that he only worked with the boys. It was an exciting lesson, for after their warm-up they launched straight away into learning new dances to celebrate the Autumn Equinox, the time when the day and the night would be exactly the same length. Ruid taught with a great deal of humour and by the end of the afternoon she was surprised to find how much she had learnt while laughing and having a lot of fun.

Leaving the practice room, she walked straight into Yssa and Lyria leaving their class in the adjacent one.

"Hello Tiera," called Yssa, "Milon told me you're having some problems, is that right?"

"Yes," Tiera replied, "He said you'd all help me to sort them out after classes today."

"Of course we will," said Lyria, "We all need to go and change now, but meet us back here in half an hour."

"Thanks, I will!"

In the dorter, the other girls were drifting back from their classes and changing out of their practice clothes.

"I'm going to do my prep in the garden," said Selma, "are you coming with me Tiera?"

"Er, no, I have to meet Milon and his sister in a minute," Tiera answered.

Selma looked puzzled, but Tiera did not stop to explain. She did not know what to say to Selma, how much to tell her, so she fled the dorter and ran to find the half-fay trio.

They walked to one of the more secluded parts of the garden and settled themselves on a bench. From then until almost dinner time they took it in turns to coach Tiera in ways of shutting out unwanted thoughts. One of them would engage her in conversation while the other two deliberately tried to put thoughts into her head. Silly thoughts that might make her laugh, embarrassing thoughts guaranteed to make her blush. They all knew that this would be far harder to block out than ordinary conversation and that if she could shut it all out, she should have no difficulty at mealtimes or in any crowd.

By the time they had to go indoors for the evening meal she felt exhausted with the effort, but when she sat down at table, and realised that she could, indeed, have an ordinary conversation without being bombarded by uninvited thoughts, she was grateful for the time her friends had spent teaching her.

Even so, dinner was not easy. Selma, who was sitting further up the table with Bron, looked curiously at Tiera time and time again, and she had the distinct feeling that they were talking about her. Suddenly, she realised that she could tune in to their thoughts if she wanted to and was tempted. But no, she said to herself, that would not be good. It would not be the right way to use her new-found gifts. Instead, she rushed away from the table the minute the meal was over, flew to the dorter to collect some books then back to the girls' sitting room where she buried herself in a corner and concentrated on her book in a way that deterred anybody from speaking to her. After an hour or so she went up to Blue dorter, washed and got into bed before any of the other girls came up, and pretended to be fast asleep when they did.

In the morning, though, it was impossible to avoid the other girls. Selma confronted her the minute she was out of bed.

"Tiera, what's the matter with you? What's going on?"

"Nothing's the matter. I'm perfectly alright, thank you. There's nothing 'going on' as you put it," retorted Tiera.

"Oh yes there is! You've been avoiding me, avoiding Bron, looking half-mad at meal-times and running off with people from the seniors every five minutes."

"Oh, you're exaggerating!" said Tiera, and rushed off to the bathing-room. But she knew that what Selma had said was mostly true, and she felt miserable because she did not know what to do about it. Her poor body was not happy either! She'd thrown herself into yesterday's dance classes with all her might, forgetting that she had not danced for a whole moon, and that some of the work was unfamiliar because she had, once again, been moved up a class. Now her muscles were protesting! If she hadn't been so anxious to avoid her dorter companions, she'd have asked Cassie for oils to put in her bath to ease her limbs last night, but she'd hurried into bed after a quick wash. No time to bath now, so she contented herself with rubbing her calf muscles as hard as she could, and promised herself she would get some oils from Cassie for a bath tonight.

****

In the first dance class of the day, Tama twice had to call Tiera's attention back to the exercise they were learning, and would have done so several more times, had she not seen tears welling up in the girl's eyes the second time. When the class ended she hurried to the next room where she knew that Muria would also have just finished teaching. Without preamble she said to her,

"Do you know what's the matter with Tiera? Something's clearly troubling her."

"Ah, I was afraid there might be difficulties when the rest of the students got back from the summer break. She's found out that she's half-fay, as I suspected from the beginning and she's discovering some of her powers. They were easy enough to manage when there was hardly anybody here, and those who were, were mostly half-fay too. In fact, Lyria and Yssa and her brother have been really helpful to her. But I think I'd better have a word with her myself. Do you know where she is?"

"If we're quick, we may find her still in the changing room. I'll go and look."

Tiera was, indeed, still in the changing room, sitting in a corner still in her practice dress and quietly crying. Tama put a hand gently on her shoulder and said,

"Muria wants to talk to you. She's in the room next door."

So Tiera wiped her eyes - something she seemed to be doing far too often these days - and went with Tama.

"Tiera, what lesson do you have next?" asked Muria.

"History," sniffed Tiera.

"I think you can be excused history just for today. It feels rather more important that you and I have a talk. I'll send a message across. Now, go and change out of your dance clothes and come over to my study, there's a good girl."

****

Later, in her study, Muria said,

"I think I can guess what's troubling you, Tiera: you can hear everybody's thoughts and you're finding it difficult to handle. Am I right?"

"It's not that so much, because Milon and Yssa and Lyria spent the whole of yesterday evening teaching me how to shut out what I don't want to hear. It's more that Selma and the others think I'm acting strange and I don't know what to tell them. I mean, am I allowed to tell them I am a half-fay or are we supposed to keep quiet about it?"

"I think it will become known sooner or later," said Muria softly, "It is not a good idea to boast about the fact, or about your special gifts, but if you are asked directly you should tell the truth. Would you like me to talk to Selma? It might be easier for you than telling her yourself."

"Oh, thank you! That would be wonderful. I mean, I felt embarrassed at the idea of telling any of the others even if I was allowed to. I thought it would sound as if I was showing off."

"Then I shall do that some time today and you are to come straight to me if the situation causes any more problems between you and your friends."

"Thank you so much, Muria, I will."

"Then run off now and don't worry any more." But privately, Muria suspected that would not be the end of the matter. Despite what she had said to Tiera just a week or two earlier about half-fays finding it easier to live among the Dancers than in society generally, she knew that even here it would not be entirely without difficulties. She had watched other half-fay children trying to adjust to being a little different from their peers, and she remembered, only too vividly, her own childhood and apprenticeship. Sometimes she wondered whether the gifts they shared were an adequate reward for the sense of being a little apart. Then she shook herself and told herself not to be so melancholy. Of course it was all worth while, and she was certain that Tiera would find that was true in the end.

CHAPTER ELEVEN

In the dorter after the afternoon classes, Tiera was mobbed.

"Oh, you are such a silly-billy!" exclaimed Selma, hugging her fit to break all her bones, "There we were, thinking something awful was wrong, and instead of that, it was something wonderful. Why didn't you tell us?"

"Well, I'm not sure that it's wonderful - I'm finding it very confusing! And I felt shy about telling you, so Muria thought it would be easier if she did so."

"Tell us what's been happening," said Ambla.

"Yes, all the details," said Emmi.

"Well, I was in the garden on the first day of the holidays, and this squirrel came and talked to me! It gave me a message I had to take to Muria at once. So then Muria told me that she reckoned I was a half-fay, and that Yssa and Milon and Lyria were, too. That's really all."

"And is it true that you know what people are

thinking?" asked Jekka.

"Only if I try to. At first I could hear everyone all the time, but Milon and Yssa and Lyria have been teaching me how to stop that happening."

"Oh!" said Selma, "So that's what you were doing with Milon the other evening. Bron was upset, you know. Jealous," she giggled, then added more seriously, "I was a bit jealous of you running off with the three of them, too, especially when I'd just got back from the holidays."

"Oh, Selma, you'll always be my best friend, but I'm sure you understand I might need to talk to other people like myself sometimes."

"Of course I will," said Selma, giving her another hug.

Tiera went to sleep with a light heart, and excelled herself in the morning dance class, but she soon found that the problem was not as quickly dealt as that. Bron was very distant when they found themselves side by side at the lunch table, and when she tackled him about it on their way out of the refectory, he said, huffily,

"I can understand Milon was helping you with

something, but I can't see that he needed to put his arm round you to do so!"

"Oh, Bron! Don't be silly. It was just a friendly gesture." But Tiera remembered reading Milon's mind when he was thinking 'Tiera is very pretty,' and blushed. And Bron noticed.

Ruid's class soon diverted her from such thoughts, though. There were only a few weeks until the Autumn Equinox, and they had to work hard at learning the new dances.

"At the Autumn Equinox we celebrate the richness of nature," Ruid explained when he allowed them a few minutes to get their breath back, "We give thanks for all the fruits and grain and other good things that have ripened over the summer, but we also prepare for the slowing down of Autumn, when the trees shed their leaves and many plants go underground ready for Winter. Our dances have to express all that." And they set to work again to memorise the movements he had devised for that purpose.

As always on the Equinoxes, there were two sets of dances to be learnt: a private dance to be done in the forest clearing at dawn and another to be performed more publicly in the city. Tiera looked forward especially to the first, for she hoped to see the Lady Titania, the Green Lord and their retinue again. Now that she knew who they were, and her own links to the fairy world, it made the prospect even more exciting and the threw herself body and soul into the rehearsal.

When the class was finished, Ruid said to her,

"Well done, Tiera. When you've changed, will you go to Muria, she has something to tell you."

In Muria's study, she found Lyria, Yssa and Milon waiting, too.

"Ah, Tiera, I thought I'd wait until you were here so I need only read this once," said Muria, "I have a message from Lord Therron that you should all hear. She unrolled a scroll and began to read:

'Dear First Dancer Muria,

'I am writing to tell you that my men have reported on the matter of illegal logging in the Sacred Forest that you and your young people so rightly drew to my attention.

I sent a party of four foresters and two dozen

guards, twice as many as on the first occasion. After some searching, for it was well hidden, they discovered an encampment of at least 20 men, with machinery and mules for transporting timber and a large area of forest clear-cut. Most of the loggers fled as soon as my men got near, which in itself shows that they knew they were doing wrong. Those who did not get away were questioned, and all told the same story: that they were in the pay of Lord Yevon and cutting trees on his orders.

'Accordingly, I sent orders to Lord Yevon to present himself at my court in Allegria. He claimed to need timber for pit-props (his lands are indeed rich in minerals). I have imposed a fine of ten thousand scudos for damaging the Sacred Forest and a sworn promise that he will take no more wood from the Forest and replant the cut areas immediately.

'I send my sincere thanks to yourself and the four young people involved for having helped us avoid worse damage.

'Yours most cordially, Therron.'

"Wow! That's great," said Milon, "There shouldn't

be any more trouble now."

****

At the great door of Castle Yevon, the Lord of that name wiped the sweat from his face, and shrugged off his travelling cape.

"Well?" said the Lady Khoda, even before he was inside, "I hope you did nothing that is going to stop these miners of yours searching for the geode, *my* geode. Heaven knows it's taking them long enough."

"Just let me get indoors and sit down," puffed her husband, "I need a drink. I've ridden a long way today."

"Pity the poor horse!" retorted the Lady Khoda, looking pointedly at her husband as he sank his oversized frame into his favourite chair. He ignored her and called,

"Quar, bring drinks!"

"Yes, m'lord," said Quar who was already on his way into the hall with a loaded tray.

"Well, tell me what happened," said Lady Khoda without even waiting for Quar to leave them, "I hope you didn't let that wretched Therron put the wind up you. Not that it would surprise me, milksop that you are."

"He *is* the ruler of all Kerran ... ," Lord Yevon began.

"And by what right? Only because your great-grandfather was an even bigger wimp than you are!" sneered his wife, "If he'd had any guts Swathia would still be an independent state. Well, once I have my hands on that geode, it will be again, just you wait and see. And more: Therron and his like will be bowing and scraping to us, as they would have done all along if your great-great-great-grandfather, or whoever it was, had kept the Great Geode here, instead of letting it be carted off to Allegria, But tell me what happened at Therron's."

"Well, he didn't give me a lot of choice..."

The Lady Khoda sighed loudly.

"... I had to promise to stop cutting trees....."

"Oh, you *idiot*. Now how are we going to manage the mining?"

"My dear, we have enough pit-props to start. Wilkin and his men are already tunnelling towards the big cave. If we need any more I can buy timber from the wharves in the harbour."

"Huh! That'll double the costs."

"Does that matter if we find the geode you want?"

"Well I'm glad you see it that way!" said the Lady Khoda, "but I don't like that word 'if'. There is no *if* about it. You find me that geode or I'll leave here. I won't just leave you, I'll leave these miserable mountains and go somewhere warm. And I've no doubt I'll find a more amenable husband there when I do."

Lord Yevon did not reply. A very wicked thought was creeping into his head - that it would be quite a relief if she did! But he did not have the nerve to say so.

"I'm going to bed," announced the Lady Khoda, "and in the morning you can take me to see the mines."

Lord Yevon poured himself another drink, a large

one. He had not dared tell his wife about the fine, but he was certain that Wilkin would find more than ten thousand scudos' worth of crystals once the mining began in earnest. The trouble was, it hadn't! Wilkin and his men were tunnelling every day, but they hadn't got anywhere near the Great Chamber, and that was the only place, or so they said, that a large geode might be found. What he could show his wife in the morning, he had no idea. Miserably, he went off to his bed.

****

The day of the Autumn Equinox arrived, and the Dancers were up before dawn and dressed in warm clothes ready for their celebration in the forest clearing. As soon as they had all had a warming drink, at Cassie's insistence, they set off through the gardens and along the little path that led to the clearing, carrying baskets of nuts and berries, acorns and wild apples for the forest creatures.

They were barely in the clearing before Tiera saw the Lady Titania in the shadows just beyond the first ring of trees, the Green Lord next to her and a whole host of fairies and elves around them. As soon as the dance began, they glided out of the shadows and spun in and out between the human dancers. Tiera caught Milon's eye and knew from his smile that he saw them, too. She was sure all the half-fays could see them, but Muria had said something once about other people, full humans, who could see them too. She wondered who they might be but could not ponder on it because it was time for her class to move into the centre of the clearing and perform the dance Ruid had taught them. Then came the final dance, involving every Dancer, and the scattering of the nuts and fruits for the forest creatures.

On the path back to the Hall, Grammi caught up with her and asked who the other people were who'd been dancing with them. "Ah!" thought Tiera, "Here's one answer to my question."

"What did they look like? she asked, though she could guess very well what the answer would be.

"There was a beautiful lady," said Grammi, "and a man with green clothes, and lots of other people who I've not seen before. They were dancing very beautifully, but they are not from Dancers' Hall."

"They are the fairies, their Queen and the King of the Forest," Tiera said. "Have you told Muria about them?"

"No," said the younger girl.

"Well, I would if I were you," said Tiera.

Then it was time for a quick breakfast before processing into the city for the more public part of the day's celebrations.

Once again, they carried baskets of food, but this time they were full of grain and vegetables from the farms outside the city, loaves from the bakers, bunches of grapes from the vineyards, and flagons of wine made from last year's grapes. They carried them to the Temple, where they laid them on the altar as part of their dance. The ceremony was in many ways similar to the one they had performed at Midsummer, though less people came to watch at this time of year. They laid all their offerings in the centre of the courtyard, and formed a circle round them before going into the wild, twirling and leaping dances that Ruid and the other teachers had made especially for the occasion. Then those chosen (and Tiera was not one of them this time) carried the baskets of offerings to lay on the altar.

Ruid had explained during rehearsals that the offerings, and a great deal more food besides, would be given away later in the day to the poorer people of the city. Some would come to the Temple to receive their gifts, and the priestesses would take food to the homes of the elderly and sick who could not.

Cassie, as always on the major festivals of the year, had produced a feast for them when they got back from the Temple. Minna and Nessa had decorated the tables with ears of wheat and bunches of berries, and while the Dancers were seating themselves, they carried in steaming bowls of Cassie's special pumpkin soup.

"Yummy!" said Bron, tucking in, "Dancing out of doors in this weather certainly gives you an appetite!" When he'd cleared his bowl and wiped up the very last drops with a hunk of home-made bread, he sat back to wait for the next course and said,

"Well, now there's only one more major Festival to celebrate this year."

"Which one is that?" asked Tiera, for she had not

been taught about the great festivals that mark the seasons before she came to Dancers' Hall.

"Why, it's the Winter Solstice, of course," said Bron, surprised that anybody should not know that. "You know, the Midwinter Festival of Lights."

"Oh!" exclaimed Tiera, "That's my birthday! It's the only Festival I knew before I came here. When Mama was alive we used to go to watch the procession every year, and I got my birthday presents on the same day."

"Do any of the teachers know that?" asked Selma.

"No, I don't think so. It's never been discussed. I said I would be thirteen in the winter, that was all."

"Well, you'd better tell somebody! At least let Cassie know, or you won't get a cake!"

CHAPTER TWELVE

The wheel of the year had moved on and now it was true winter. Frost dusted the gardens with sparkling white every morning and beyond them the trees at the edge of the Sacred Forest glistened. Hurrying between the Hall and the teaching block, the students could see their breath hanging in the air.

Rehearsals for the Winter Solstice were well under way and Cassie and her helpers were busy sorting out costumes for the day; red woollen leggings for the girls and women, forest green ones for the men and boys, matching hats and gloves and contrasting tunics of warm woollen felt for everyone. They all had to be unwrapped from the camphor-wood chests where they'd lain since last winter, tried on for size, altered if needs be. Some people still fitted into the clothes they'd worn last year but many had grown taller, and of course there were the new young dancers who had never taken part in a winter festival before.

Tiera stood in Cassie's laundry room waiting her

turn to be fitted. Nessa and Minna were helping the younger children to pull on the tight leggings amid a lot of laughter. Cassie hurried across to Tiera with an armful of green and red and said,

"Well, you're a problem, my chick, you really are!"

"Why? What have I done wrong?"

"It's nothing you've done, chick, it's just that I'm having trouble finding anything to fit you. You see, most people who haven't done the Midwinter dances before are a whole lot younger than you. Still, I think I've got something sorted now; try this lot on and let's see what you look like."

So Tiera tried on the leggings: they fitted, and a tunic which was fine, too. The hat and gloves were no problem, but boots? Oh dear! She could barely get her feet down the upper part, let alone into the shoe itself. It took four more tries before they found a pair in which she was comfortable. They needed, after all, to be a perfect fit because she had to dance in them. There could be no question of settling for a size too big and wearing an extra pair of socks!

Now she had to really hurry to get to the practice

room where they were to have a dress rehearsal. If there hadn't been so much frost on the grass Ruid would have preferred to hold this last rehearsal on the lawn, but to have so many people stamp about on it now would damage the grass, so he turned off the heating and opened all the windows to prevent the Dancers getting overheated.

Even so, Tiera felt very strange dancing in so many clothes, though they left the gloves and hats off while they practised. After a first run-through, they did the whole dance again with the lanterns that they would be carrying in the Festival, the only difference being that today they were not lit. By the end, they were all bathed in sweat despite the open windows and absence of heating, but nobody grumbled, because they knew they would be more than glad of the layers of wool at dawn tomorrow. Then Ruid had them all sit down while he gave out final instructions about the handling of the lanterns.

"Now listen carefully, I'm not going to say this again - there won't be time - and I don't want any accidents. This is the Festival of Lights, not the Festival of Setting Ourselves Alight!"

The older students groaned: they'd heard the same joke year in and year out for as long as they had been at Dancers' Hall! But he was going on. Those carrying lanterns on poles were to be extremely careful about planting them firmly in the ground; those who were to hang their lantern on a tree were to be sure the branch was thick enough to hold it; nobody was to carry bare candles, they must all be enclosed in a glass lantern; if a lantern broke, they were to blow out the candle at once, and on and on and on. Most of them had heard it all before, but Tiera and the youngsters who'd been promoted at the same time as her took it all very seriously. Then it was time to go and change and hang up their costumes ready for the morrow.

When Tiera got back to the dorter there was a lot of scuffling and whispering, but she was too busy struggling out of her costume to take much notice. Then there was a mad rush to the bathing-rooms; everybody wanted to bath at the same time after such a sweaty rehearsal but some had to wait, for there were more girls than baths. Finally, it was time for dinner, served early because of tomorrow's early start, and an early bedtime for the same reason.

****

Dawn comes late in mid-winter, and it was still pitch dark when Tiera woke to a chorus of "Happy Birthday"! Minna, who was doing the round of the dorters waking everybody ready for the dawn celebrations, turned on the light, revealing a pile of packages at the foot of Tiera's bed.

"Oh!" she exclaimed, sitting up and rubbing her eyes.

"Happy Birthday", the five other girls sang out, but Minna, before hastening off to wake up Green Dorm, said,

"Be quick girls, you need to be in costume and downstairs as fast as you can. I don't think you've got time to open parcels."

There was a collective groan, "Oh, spoilsport," somebody muttered, though they knew she was out of earshot.

166

"Never mind," it will be even more fun later," said Ambla, as they scrambled to get washed and helped each other into their costumes.

As always on the days of dawn celebrations, Cassie had hot drinks waiting before they went out: steaming mugs of spiced chocolate served with admonitions not to spill it on their tunics!

Then they were off, Ruid standing by the main doors to light each person's lantern before they set off two by two towards the clearing.

The flames from their candles reflected a thousandfold from the frost and icicles all around. Somebody had brushed snow away from the space where they would dance, but everywhere else it lay thick and pristine. The glade was always a magical place, but today more than ever, and between the trees Tiera saw tiny faerie lanterns echoing their own. Following Ruid's instructions, she planted her lantern firmly in the ground at the edge of the clearing, a far from easy task for it was hard frozen, then went towards the centre ready to dance.

The drum began the music, then the flute, and

finally a tinkling of bells that had not been included at rehearsals. Surrounded by the flickering lanterns they twisted and twirled, echoing the dance of snowflakes in the wind. Once again, those who could see them knew that the Green Lord and the fairy Queen and her retinue were dancing with them, and even those who could not see them felt an extra magic in the air. Looking around, Tiera could see nobody playing bells and realised, suddenly, that it was faerie music. Then the first shafts of sunlight broke through the trees, turning the ice and snow a glistening pink. Everybody there stood still and hushed to watch the magic moment. Then, as the sun rose higher and the pink faded, the human dancers ended their celebration and their forest friends melted into the air. Gathering up their lanterns, the Dancers made their way back to what they knew would be a late but extra-special breakfast.

Once indoor, there was a scramble to get out of costumes and back to the refectory where their expectations were more than met: there were steaming piles of pancakes on the tables, jugs of syrup and half a dozen different kinds of jam to spread on them, and as fast as hungry dancers cleared their plates, Minna, Nessa and Cassie carried in more, followed by jugs of hot, spiced apple juice. When everybody had been served with juice, Ruid stood up and rapped on the top table for silence.

"Let's drink a toast to Cassie!" he said, "All year round she feeds us delicious and nourishing food, but on the festival days she excels herself. I think that's the best breakfast I've had for a year."

"Here, here!" agreed a score of voices, though at the same time there was a lot of laughter.

They all raised their mugs and yelled "To Cassie!" while she stood at the bottom of the steps, blushing and smiling from ear to ear.

"Thanks, everybody," she said, "I try my best to keep your bodies and souls together!"

"Why were people laughing?" Tiera asked Selma.

"Because it's another of Ruid's ancient jokes. We always have pancakes for breakfast on the Winter Solstice, and he always says it's the best breakfast he's had for a year."

"I see!" said Tiera, laughing as well.

Now they had some free time and Selma and Jekka grabbed Tiera's arms and ushered her up to the girls' sitting room. They sat Tiera down in an armchair and, one by one, presented her with little packages. There was a mirror and comb from Ambla, a book from Jekka, another book from Emmi - they knew how much Tiera loved reading now, after her earlier struggles. Winna's gift was a box of sweetmeats, and Breda's a selection of hair-ribbons. Finally, Selma handed her a mysteriously lumpy package, which Tiera poked and prodded amid much giggling, trying to guess what might be inside.

"I give up!" she laughed at last, tearing off the paper to reveal a dog made of plush.

"Oh, he's adorable!" she cried.

"I made him in craft class," Selma said proudly.

A group of girls from Green dorter had been half-watching from the other side of the room while trying to give the impression of not being really interested. Now Crissa got up and walked across to where Tiera was hugging her new dog, and said,

"Ugh, what an ugly brute! Look, it's cross-eyed, and

one ear's a different shape from the other."

"I don't care. I love him anyway. He's got character," said Tiera, fiercely defending her best friend's handiwork, "I'm going to call him Flip."

"Though even if it were perfect, I'd have thought you were too old for stuffed toys," sneered Crissa, making her way back to her cronies.

Tiera said nothing but, suddenly, she had a piercing glimpse of Crissa's mind. A little voice was whispering 'I've never had a toy dog. Not even when I was little,' and Tiera knew that behind the sneering exterior Crissa was a very unhappy girl. She was wondering what to do with this new knowledge, whether to say anything to Crissa, when Nessa popped her head round the door and said,

"Cassie says you're all to go and lie down for an hour or so because it's going to be a late night. There'll be high tea at five instead of dinner today."

They all groaned, and reluctantly straggled off to their various dorters. Nobody really slept, the prospect of the lantern-lit procession and the big bonfire was too exciting.

When tea-time came, Tiera's friends whispered on the way downstairs and once they arrived at their usual table, Tiera saw why: a cake with 13 candles was waiting for them. And that was not all. They were just sitting down, jostling for who sat nearest the cake, when Emmi nudged Tiera and pointed towards the door.

"Look who's here,' she said.

Tiera turned round, and there in the doorway stood Dilla and Frol, with their foster-mother, Beatta. Tiera jumped up and ran to hug them, as Cassie appeared through the other door and joined them.

"Come on in," she said, "Come and sit at Tiera's table - I think if the girls squeeze up a bit we can pop these two little ones in," and she ushered them into the hall, among some curious looks - it was not often that non-dancers ate with them.

Tea was as delicious as breakfast, and finally Cassie came and lit the candles on the cake, Tiera blew them out and Cassie cut slices for everyone at her table. Nobody else needed to be envious, though, as she had provided similar cakes for all the other tables, though without candles. Then it was time to go and get back into dance costumes again. Tiera gave Dilla and Frol huge hugs, and another for Beatta who she had grown very fond of over the summer.

****

The procession through Allegria was truly spectacular. The Dancers were not the only people carrying lanterns that night; every guild in the city sent groups with lights of some kind or another to mark the shortest day. In the place of honour at the front of the procession were the candle-makers, for without them nobody else would have lights at all. The leading men carried a huge lantern in the shape of the Sun, swinging from a pole high above their heads, and behind them came others almost as large, representing the Moon and stars. Behind them came the line of Dancers and after them the weavers, spinners, tailors, the grocers, winemakers and bakers, the builders, shipwrights and smiths and men and women from every profession you could name.

The streets were packed with folk eager to see the spectacle, though once the parade had passed, most people hurried on towards the great central square, for here the bonfire would be lit once the procession arrived. The crowd here was dense and growing all the time, though a ring of Vigiles made sure that a space was kept clear in the middle. Excitement mounted as the candlemakers' great lanterns came into view, followed by the great snaking line of lights behind them. Filing into the square, they made a circle between the fire - as yet unlit - and the cordon of Vigiles.

Now came the sound of trumpets, and a formation of Lord Therron's personal guards came into view, and behind them, Lord Therron himself with Lady Helma and members of his family. There were cheers as he climbed up to a platform near the fire, for he was a just ruler and genuinely loved.

"People of Allegria, people of Kerran, greetings to you on this Winter Solstice!" his voice rang out. "I know you haven't come here to listen to me! We've all come to mark the shortest day and the longest night, the darkest time of the year, and remind ourselves that the year is on the turn, and the Sun will come back as strong as ever before long. So, I won't waste any more of your time!" and he threw a flaming brand into the fire as he climbed down from the platform.

Once the flames had gained a hold, and the whole pile was glowing, it was time for the ceremonial dance. The Dancers joined hands and began to circle the fire, singing an age-old chant. Gradually other voices took up the tune, and other circles formed outside theirs, moving always in a clockwise direction round the fire. Tiera remembered that Muria had told them, in a history lesson, that hundreds of years ago people thought that the Sun moved round the Earth, and the dance was meant to strengthen him on his journey. Even though they knew now that the Earth moved round the Sun, it felt good to preserve the ancient songs and dances. On and on they went, circling the fire as it gradually burned down until a trumpet sounded, and in the silence that followed Lord Therron's voice rang out over the square.

"Good night, good citizens, and an auspicious year to you all!"

****

Tiera fell asleep that night thinking "This is the best birthday I have ever had."

CHAPTER THIRTEEN

It was Springtime. A whole year had passed since Tiera arrived at Dancers' Hall and the routines of a dance student's life had become second nature to her. It was a normal afternoon; dance classes had just finished and students were making their way back to the dorters to change, or gossiping in the gardens, when a horseman staggered into the grounds.

"Where can I find your First Dancer?" he gasped, grabbing hold of Baldor, who was the first person he met inside the main gate.

"You mean Muria," said the boy, "She'll have just finished teaching for the day, so she may be in her study, or she may still be in one of the practice rooms." Baldor stopped a younger boy who was on his way back to the house.

"Kay," he said, "run back to the practice block and see if Muria's still there. If she is, tell her there's a gentleman who wants to see her urgently. If not, try her study then come back and let me know quickly."

As Kay sped off, Baldor turned to the stranger and asked,

"Is there anything I can do to help in the meantime?"

"Yes, some water for my horse!"

Baldor looked around for another messenger, and spied Grammi and Petra gossiping nearby.

"Petra! Grammi! Here, I've got an errand for you, it's urgent. I want you to run to the Sanctuary and find Cassie, or Nessa or Minna if she isn't there, and ask if you can borrow a bucket, then bring it back here with water for this gentleman's horse."

The girls stared curiously at the sweaty, mud-caked man then scampered off towards the Sanctuary.

"What brings you here in such haste?" asked Baldor, while they waited for the younger students to return.

"I've come from the Lord Felsal. His wife and child are very ill. They need help, and quickly. I've ridden all night and most of today to get here."

Just then, they saw Kay and Muria hurrying in their direction from the practice rooms and the rider ran towards them. As soon as he reached them the messenger blurted out the same news that he had just told Baldor, adding that the Lady Bethna had given birth too soon, and both she and the baby were in grievous danger.

"Oh! That is awful. Of course we will help. Come with me. We must think what is the best course of action," and she led him towards her study. At almost the same time, Minna came from the direction of the sanctuary lugging a bucket of water, with Grammi and Petra close behind.

"Where's this horse?" she puffed.

"Tethered just outside the main gate," the rider called back over his shoulder, "Please would somebody take his blanket from the saddle-bag and cover him before he takes a chill? Thank you, that would be so kind," then he followed Muria into the house.

"Sit down, tell me exactly what happened," said Muria as she led the man into her study.

"The Lady Bethna gave birth to a baby boy, her first child, but he came before his time. He should not have been born for another moon at least, and he's too weak to suckle, even if my lady had milk to give him. The wise-women found a wet-nurse for him but he barely swallows and they fear he will not live. And now they dread that child-bed fever may kill my lady. Lord Felsal is beside himself with anxiety. The physicians have tried everything they know, but my lady keeps asking for the Dancers. She believes a healing dance is the only thing that will save her child. As for herself, I think she does not realise how ill she is, but Lord Felsal does and he begs for a healing dance for her, also."

"Of course, of course. We'll send a party as soon as I can organise it, but how long would it take us to reach Lord Felsal's?"

"I would think two days at the very least, riding as fast as possible. I've ridden a day and a night, scarcely stopping but it's near done for my horse."

"You realise that hardly any of our dancers know how to ride? And we have no horses; we do not have any need of horses in normal circumstances."

"My Lord Felsal realises that, lady, and he has sent me with money to hire mounts. Just as soon as you can tell me how many riders, I am to see to that."

"I must think who it would be best to send. Let me arrange for some refreshment for you while I gather my colleagues together, you must be in sore need of it."

"You are kind, lady, but I must first see to my horse. Once I have done that I would be more than glad of food and drink."

Tama, Allya and Ruid, called hastily to Muria's rooms, considered the crisis.

"Ruid, you're the only one of us four who can ride a horse," said Muria, "and in any case I feel we should send somebody senior."

"I'll go, and willingly, but who else should I take with me? Four is the absolute minimum number of dancers we'd need for a healing dance."

"Yes, and the other three should be women, I feel," said Muria, "Tama, will you go?"

"I'd go, but I've never ridden a horse in my life! And clearly to hire a carriage would make the journey far too slow."

"We could get a groom to ride with you before him in the saddle."

"Very well, I'll go."

"Then we need two more, and one of them needs to be a half-fay. I can't send Liana - we can hardly spare any more staff, so it had better be senior girls," mused Muria, "Verla would be a good choice, she's sensible, doesn't panic, and I think Tiera should be the other. We'd have to get grooms to ride with them, too."

"Why Tiera? Why not Yssa or Lyria?" asked Allya.

"Those two are completely comfortable with their gifts. Tiera isn't entirely so yet and it would do her good to discover how she can use them for the greatest good."

The others nodded, understanding.

"How long is all this going to take? Hiring horses and grooms, I mean," asked Allya, "What I am thinking is that perhaps we should perform a distant healing even before we leave here."

"Allya, you are so wise," said Muria, "Can I leave you to organise that while I talk to Lord Felsal's messenger?"

"I'll deal with the messenger," said Ruid, "I can go with him to the nearest stables and see what we can arrange while you talk to Verla and Tiera."

"Thank you, Ruid, so much."

****

Within the hour, Allya had assembled musicians and most of the senior students in the Sanctuary. Muria and Tama joined them but without Ruid who had gone with Torm - for that was the messenger's name - to the stables. None of the students had taken part in an absent healing before, but Muria explained that they would do a healing dance in the usual way, except that instead of a person on the couch, they were to hold the names of Lady Bethna and Ildon, the baby boy, in their minds throughout the dance. Then the candles were lit, and they went into the Inner Sanctuary to begin their healing work.

Cassie, meanwhile, searched her cupboards for travelling clothes, not something the Dancers needed very often. But she drew on her stock of winter things for cloaks to wrap them at night, and boys' breeches that she thought the girls had better wear, however unladylike! Then she turned her thoughts to food for the journey. By the time Ruid and the Torm came back from the stables, everything was arranged.

It turned out, though, that no grooms would be available until morning.

"Just as well," thought Cassie, "that man looks as if he could do with a good sleep."

****

It was still completely dark when the party left Dancers' Hall. Led by Ruid, they made their way to the stables and were introduced to the grooms who would ride with them, while their belongings were stowed in the saddle-bags. Despite the serious reason for their journey, Tiera and Verla were tempted to giggle because they felt so odd in their boys' clothes but they comforted themselves with the thought that their normal clothes, and robes for the dance, were stowed in the bags.

Then the grooms lifted them into the saddles, sprung up behind them and they were off.

The first day's journey was uneventful. They rode

steadily, stopping only to eat and rest the horses around noon. With three of the horses carrying two people each, it was impossible to gallop, but towards evening Torm spurred his horse ahead in order to find lodgings for them all at an inn. There they ate supper and went to bed early, to be ready for a dawn start the next day. The morning passed much as it had done on the first day, but after their noon rest the road became steeper and their progress slower as they reached the foothills of the mountains that surrounded Lord Felsal's lands.

It was clear that Torm was becoming more and more anxious as the day wore on, but as the road grew ever steeper it was impossible for the horses to move any faster. Indeed, the grooms dismounted and led the three horses carrying Tama, Tiera and Verla to spare them a little on the steep ascent. By late afternoon it was clear that they could not possibly reach Castle Felsal before dark and Torm, once again, galloped ahead to look for lodgings.

This time, though, he had less success; the only inn within reach was full, and all the innkeeper could offer them was space in hayloft above the stables. When they'd eaten a bowl of thin soup apiece, they climbed up into the loft and made nests in the hay, wrapping themselves gratefully in the thick cloaks that Cassie had insisted on packing. They slept fitfully, and rose at dawn once again to set out on what must surely be the final part of their journey.

Mercifully, they did not have to climb much further. Before it was fully light, they were on the road that led down into the valleys and by the middle of the morning they could see Castle Felsal below them. For the last time, Torm rode on ahead, and by the time the Dancers reached the castle, the drawbridge had been lowered, grooms were standing ready to tend to their horses and Lord Felsal himself waiting to greet them.

"How glad I am to see you! How grateful," he cried as he grasped Ruid's hands, "though my good lady and our son have improved a little since I sent Torm speeding to beg your help. I feared then that you might arrive only to officiate at a burial. But the fever left my lady two nights back, and the babe has seemed a little stronger since then, too."

"I am glad of that," replied Ruid, "and now that we

are here, we will do all that we can to help them towards full health."

"Thank you, thank you. Now, introduce me to your fellow-dancers."

Tama, Verla and Tiera stepped forward to meet the man who had called for their help. Tiera, as he shook her hand, thought that he looked one of the kindest people she had ever met - outside Dancers' Hall, that is. Even though he looked haggard from worry and lack of sleep, the creases round his brown eyes spoke of laughter.

"Come inside, all of you, my steward will find refreshment for you, and then I will take you to the Lady Bethna and our child."

****

The Lady Bethna lay in a vast, canopied bed. "She looks so small and frail in the middle of it," thought Tiera. Her face was pale, her hands lay listlessly on the silken sheets, and her eyes were closed as if she was asleep, but she opened them as she heard people

187

coming into the room.

"Is it the Dancers? Have they arrived at last?" she whispered.

"Yes my love, they are here," said Lord Felsal, taking one limp hand and kissing it.

"Then I think our son will live," she murmured.

The baby boy lay in a gilded cradle beside the great bed. The room was full of nursemaids, wise-women, apothecaries, servants and it was dark: although it was the middle of the day, great velvet curtains drawn over all the windows. Ruid took in the scene at a glance and said,

"If we are to help at all, we need light and space. Lord Felsal, it is possible for us to see the lady alone - apart from your good self, of course?"

Immediately, Lord Felsal ordered the room to be emptied, and the crush of people went out, some of them mumbling crossly as they went. Ruid and Tama went to the windows and drew back the heavy drapery, allowing sunshine to flood into the room. Lady Bethna opened her eyes, blinked and whispered,

"Give me my child."

Lord Felsal bent and, with infinite care, lifted the tiny creature from the cradle and handed him to his mother.

"Ildon, my babe, the Dancers are here, you are safe," she murmured in his ear.

The Dancers stood silent for a while, allowing her the pleasure of holding her son until Tama finally asked, very softly, if she might take the child for a moment. Laying him gently on the end of the bed, she gestured to Ruid and the two girls to help her. Ruid took the tiny feet in his hands and Tama asked Tiera to place her hands by the fragile head.

"Me?" queried Tiera.

"Yes, you are the only half-fay among us. We need you to listen to his thoughts."

So Tiera took up her position while Verla and Tama moved one on each side of the baby and held their hands over him.

The child's thoughts were faint, difficult to put into words. Tiera realised in a rush that a babe who could not yet speak would hardly think in terms of words! Yet somehow she knew. After a moment, she lifted her head and smiled,

"He wants to live! she said.

"His organs are all sound, even though they are so small," said Ruid.

"His blood is good," said Tama, "It moves well through his veins.

"His breath is getting stronger all the time," said Verla.

"Praise all the Gods!" said Lord Felsal, "Did you hear that, my beloved?"

"Yes, I heard," said his wife.

"We need to do the same for your Lady," said Ruid, and between them Tama, Ruid and Lord Felsal gently lifted her until she was laying sideways across the foot of the bed so that the Dancers could take up their positions around her.

Once again, they tuned themselves to her body and mind.

"Her love for you and your child is so great that she will recover," said Tiera after a few moments.

"She needs time to heal, but her body is strong enough to do so," said Ruid.

"She has lost blood. She needs good foods," said Verla.

"She wants so much to feed her child that her milk will flow in another day," said Tama, standing up. "Now we must consider where we can dance for them. Let her rest until then.

CHAPTER FOURTEEN

The Dancers walked in the walled yard outside the castle, Ruid a little ahead discussing with Lord Felsal where best to perform the healing dance, Tama and the two girls following a few steps behind. Tiera looked around her and up at the towers and turrets. What a strange place, she thought. It was unlike any building in Allegria.

"I wouldn't like to live in a place like this at all: too dark, too shut in," she said to Verla, although beyond the moat she could see beautiful meadows and wooded hillsides.

"Me neither," agreed Verla.

"No, it's not what we're used to at home," said Tama, "but there are good reasons why these old fortresses were made in this way. The land was still very wild when they were built - I'm not sure when, but a very long time ago - and bandits from the hills would raid the villages, steal the cattle and horses, carry off young women to be their brides and often kill the men.

The moat and high walls were made so that everybody could shelter inside and bring their cattle and horses with them."

"Well, I'm glad we live in Allegria!" said Tiera.

"Me too!" agreed Verla.

Lord Felsal and Ruid had stopped and were waiting for them to catch up.

"I think we have decided where you can best do your dance," said Lord Felsal, "If you'd like to come with me I will show you."

They made their way back into the castle and he led them to a room near Lady Bethna's bedchamber which was almost empty. It was intended, Lord Felsal said, to become a nursery for the infant Ildon.

Tiera sniffed. It smelt stale and fusty, but she saw that Ruid was already moving towards a window.

"May I open this?" he asked.

"Of course! Do whatever is needed to make the place suitable."

"Candles. It would be good to have as many of them as possible. Also a couch of some kind for your lady and the child to lie on," said Ruid.

"I will call servants and arrange it at once," said Lord Felsal, "excuse me while I go to attend to it."

So Ruid and Tama threw open all the windows and pushed what little furnishings there were back against the walls. Ruid opened one of the saddle-bags that he had brought with him, and drew out a package wrapped in silk cloth. As he carefully peeled away the layers of silk one by one, Tiera saw that he had brought with him a large amethyst, not as big as the one in the Inner Sanctuary at home and incomparably smaller than the Great Geode, but of the same kind.

"Wherever we do a healing dance, we try to have at least one amethyst with us," explained Ruid, and proceeded to take out another packet. As he unwrapped this one in turn, they saw that it contained a number of smaller amethysts.

"Here, girls, would you like to arrange these around the room? As we couldn't carry the really large ones with us, it's good to have a number of smaller ones."

By now, servants were coming in with candles, and Verla and Tiera placed each of the crystals where it would reflect light from a candle nearby. Two men carried a couch through the door and Ruid directed them to place it in the exact centre of the room. Now Tama opened her bag and drew out the same silk cloth that Tiera remembered being placed over her long ago.

"We are ready, apart from changing into our robes," she said, taking them from her bag, too, and when Lord Felsal came back to see whether the room had been arranged to their satisfaction, she dispatched him to arrange for Lady Bethna and the baby to be carried in while they changed.

Tiera had taken part in healing dances a number of times before, but always in the outer circle, while the four teachers performed the main healing movements. All the same, she had learnt the movements in class and rehearsed them many times, and so had Verla, and they understood that Tama would take the place usually occupied by Muria, Ruid would of course be in his usual position while Verla and Tiera would replace Tama and Allya.

When Lady Bethna and the baby had been carried in by Lord Felsal and two nursemaids and covered by Tama with the lilac silk, Lord Felsal said,

"I will withdraw now and leave you to your healing work."

They took up their positions round the couch. "There's something missing," thought Tiera, and realised that they had no piper. Then Tama began to sing, her sweet voice filling the room, and the dance began.

They moved slowly round the mother and child, making the ritual hand movements that Tiera knew by heart now. They fluttered their hands over the pair, they danced faster and faster, swirling and swaying until the room felt as if there were twenty dancers, not four. Then Tama's singing hushed and slowed, and they knelt round the couch in silence.

****

The Dancers had been two days at Castle Felsal now, and were full of joy to see the Lady Bethna sitting up in her great bed and nursing tiny Ildon.

"Look, I have milk and he is suckling well!" she said when Tama and the girls came to visit them that morning.

"I think we can safely leave you soon," replied Tara.

"I think you can. I feel so much stronger now, and Ildon even has some colour in his cheeks. When I think that only a day or two ago I thought we would lose him, I cannot thank you enough."

Tama did not mention that Lord Felsal had feared for her life, too. If Lady Bethna did not realise how near death she had been, it was best not to tell her. Tama was more than ever thankful that Allya had suggested a dance of absent healing on the day that Torm had arrived with his urgent message, or the outcome could have been very different. From what Lord Felsal had said it was clear that Bethna and the baby had begun to improve around the time they had performed that dance, and she felt glad to have been part of it.

After they danced the healing for Lady Bethna and the baby, Lord Felsal had asked them if they could help his mother.

"Her back and her legs give her great pain, she is cruelly bent and she can scarcely walk. She spends a great deal of time in her chamber because it pains her so much to move about, and that is a great pity because her mind is as lively as ever, and she loves company."

"Of course, we are happy to help whoever we can, whenever we can," said Ruid, and it was arranged that the old lady should be carried to the room they had prepared. Two servants carried her in, but after the dance she walked out. Standing tall, and without leaning on her stick, she went straight to Lady Bethna's bedchamber to see her new grandchild.

They had danced for the daughter of Lord Felsal's steward who had a wasting disease, and for Lady Bethna's old nurse, who was growing confused in her old age.

But they needed to think about getting back to Allegria now that their work here was done. Tama went to find Ruid and asked him to talk to Lord Felsal about horses.

Lord Felsal would not even consider horses! He would, he said, have a coach prepared to take them back to Allegria, the grooms could ride the hired horses home, and he would send messengers ahead to ensure that they had good accommodation at each inn on the way. They must stay one more night while he set all this in train, and leave in the morning.

That night, as on the previous ones, the Dancers ate with Lord Felsal in the great hall, sitting in the places of honour at the top of the table. Further down sat the higher-ranking members of his household, and beyond them some of the people who had attended the Lady Bethna since Ildon was born. At the end of the meal Lord Felsal called for a toast to their recovery and another toast of thanks to the Dancers. Everybody raised their glasses high to toast the recovery of the lady and her child, but when it came to thanking the dancers, some made but a token gesture and there was mumbling as people left the table.

Tiera and Verla soon went to the quarters they had been allotted, to prepare for the next day's journey before they went to bed, but Lord Felsal said to Tama and Ruid,

"Will you take one more glass with me? There is something I want to discuss with you."

Once they were seated on the bench in front of the

great fireplace, glasses in hand, he said,

"This has made me think very seriously. If we were in such urgent need of your help another time a messenger might reach you too late. I'm thinking that we should have a Dancers' Hall of our own, not just to serve my household, but all the people in the towns and villages. Most of them, after all, would not have messengers and fast horses at their disposal, though I would gladly lend them if needed. Some of them, indeed, will never have heard of the Dancers and your healing work until now."

"And I perceive that not all of them welcome our presence," said Ruid quietly.

"Yes, I am sorry that was made so obvious when I called for the toast," apologised Lord Felsal, "Unfortunately, people living this far from such cities as Allegria tend to cling to old ways and resent strangers. But these are my lands and it is for me to show them that new ideas can often be good ideas. I suspect that once a few people had seen an injured child or a sick wife made better, opinions would soon begin to change. Tell me, though, what do you think of such an idea?"

"It's never been done before," said Tama, "There has only ever been one Dancers' Hall, but I can see at once that it would make sense."

"We would have to think very hard indeed about how it might work," said Ruid, "We would need to ask Muria, our First Dancer, what she feels about the idea, and it could take a good deal of time to organise."

"There would be a limit to how many dancers we could spare," said Tama, "especially experienced dancers."

"Of course," said Lord Felsal, " I do not imagine that this is something that could be accomplished overnight. I merely ask that you consider the idea and, as you say, discuss it with the First Dancer. And now, I think we should all go to our beds. You will need to be on the road early tomorrow."

****

Once back at Dancers' Hall, Ruid and Tama went at once to report to Muria.

"You'd better come too, girls," Tama said, "I'm sure Muria will want to hear from you as well."

Once they had all related their experiences, Ruid mentioned the idea that the Lord Felsal had put to him. Muria listened gravely, then she said,

"This needs a great deal of thought. It's not something we could do overnight. For example, it would need quite a number of Dancers, maybe more than we could spare. We would have to send teachers and at least one half-fay."

Tama and Ruid laughed. He said,

"That's more or less exactly what we told him!"

"This needs serious consideration, but right now I need to put my mind to more immediate affairs: Yssa was in the clearing just now and she said there was a horde of animals trying to tell her something but she couldn't make head or tail of what they were saying. I'm going out to see if I can get a clearer message myself. Make yourselves comfortable and we'll talk properly when I come back."

"May I come with you?" asked Tiera, rather shyly. She did not want Muria to think she was presuming to hear as clearly as her!

"Of course you can! Come along and let's see what we can find out."

They hurried past the lawns, through the wilder parts of the garden and into the forest clearing.

"Let's sit over here," whispered Muria, pointing to a log beneath an old pine tree that the Dancers often used as a bench.

At first, Tiera could see no animals, then a pair of rabbits scuttled out from between the trees, followed by at least twenty more of them. A dozen moles followed more slowly, sniffing their way about, and they all started talking at once!

"My goodness, no wonder Yssa couldn't make sense of it!" whispered Muria in Tiera's ear, then, addressing the crowd of animals she said, "We find it hard to understand you, my friends, when you all talk together! Are there one or two who can speak for all of you?"

An elderly-looking rabbit came forward, followed by a greying mole.

"Men make burrows," said the rabbit, "Not good.

Not right. Burrows broken. Rabbits dying."

"Moles dying. Earth move. Much noise," added the mole.

"This is very serious," said Muria, "What can we do to help you?"

"Tell good master. Bad master make burrows," said the mole.

"You want us to tell Lord Therron?" Muria asked.

"Yes. He good," said the rabbit.

"Then we will do so at once," said Muria, "Thank you for confiding in us."

She rose from the log and at once the animals began to retreat into the forest. Hurrying back towards the Hall, Muria laughed,

"I'm not surprised Yssa couldn't understand them if they were all yelling at her at once! That, and the fact that the underground creatures do not speak our language as well as the tree-dwellers. But it's no joke. We'd better get a message to Lord Therron as quickly as possible. Perhaps he can make better sense of it than I can."

As they neared the Hall, she stopped suddenly and

said,

"Oh my goodness! Do you remember Lord Therron's message about the tree cutting? He mentioned that Lord Yevon wanted wood for pit-props. Mining. "Men make burrows." ... it all makes sense now. I must send a message at once."

CHAPTER FIFTEEN

Tiera trudged wearily up to Blue dorter to change out of her travelling clothes. She had sat with Verla and the grown-ups in Muria's study for a long time, recounting their experiences at Lord Felsal's until Muria suggested the two girls would like to get changed. She sensed that the adults wanted to discuss Lord Felsal's proposal for a second Dancers' Hall.

Emmi and Selma were in Blue dorter when she walked in.

"Tiera!" "You're back." "What was it like?" "Tell us everything!"

But instead of answering, Tiera stared at her bed, at the empty space where her treasured dog should be.

"Where's Flip?" she asked.

"Oh! I thought you'd taken him with you," said Selma.

"On a horse? Stuffed into a saddlebag?" Tiera giggled, but she stopped laughing abruptly and said,

"I have a good idea where he is: in Green dorter."

"You mean Crissa?" said Selma.

"Yes. Remember my birthday? She was very jealous, she really wanted that dog."

"Huh! You wouldn't have thought so from the rude remarks she made about him!" said Selma, who had not forgotten having her handiwork insulted.

"She did want him, badly. I heard her thinking," said Tiera very quietly, "I think she was being rude to cover that up."

"That's no excuse for stealing," said Emmi.

"Let's call it borrowing," said Tiera. "I'm going to go and ask for him back."

"You're getting soft!" said Selma, "I'd better come with you to make sure you don't end up giving him to Crissa for good."

"No chance of that!" said Tiera, "I'm far too fond of him."

"I'm coming too," said Emmi.

"No, I'd rather go on my own, thank you."

Crissa was at the far end of the room, but the dog was sitting on her bed, just as Tiera expected, so she picked it up and said gently,

"I hope you've enjoyed Flip's company while I was away. I'm home now, so I'd like to take him back." She was quite prepared for an acid reply from Crissa but none came. Instead, Crissa said,

"You're not angry?"

"No, why should I be? You've done me no harm, and I can see you haven't damaged Flip."

"I wouldn't dream of damaging him. He's adorable," said Crissa, and Tiera saw that tears were welling up in her eyes. She went over to where Crissa was sitting and put an arm round her shoulder.

"Crissa, if Selma hadn't given me Flip for my birthday, if she hadn't put so much work into making him, I'd give him to you. But she'd be hurt if I did, you do understand that, don't you?"

Crissa nodded and brushed the tears from her eyes.

"It's just that I never had a stuffed toy of my own, even when I was tiny."

"I know," Tiera nodded.

"How?" said Crissa, suddenly suspicious, "I've never told anybody here what it was like at home."

"I read your mind when Selma gave me the dog. I'm

sorry. I didn't mean to pry, but that day your thoughts just popped in."

"You won't tell anybody else, will you?"

"No, of course not if you don't want me to," said Tiera, "But I must go and change now, I'm still in my travelling clothes." And she gave Crissa a quick hug before picking up the dog and leaving.

On her way back to Blue Dorter, Tiera thought 'I'm going to make a dog in craft class, find out when Crissa's birthday is and give it to her for a surprise.'

****

After the time away at Lord Felsal's Tiera needed to get back into the routine of dance training. She'd learnt from experience not to overdo her efforts for the first day or two, so she worked gently but thoroughly in the classes and remembered to get oils from Cassie to put in her bath each evening and by the end of the week, she felt completely fit again. The morning classes, as always, concentrated on dance technique and the afternoon classes were given over to preparations for

May Day. This year it was Allya who was entrusted with arranging new dances, and she was half-way through teaching a sequence of steps when Lyria tapped on the door of the practise room and said,

"Muria wants to see Tiera at once. It's very urgent."

"It must be!" said Allya. Dance classes were sacrosanct. Nobody, not even Muria, called a student out in the middle of one. But Allya smiled at Tiera and signalled for her to go. Tiera threw a towel round her shoulders and, whispering her apologies as she went, followed Lyria out.

"What's the matter?" she asked as they ran across the lawn.

"The Green Lord himself has asked Muria to do something, and she wants all the half-fays at once."

Milon and his sister were already in the study when they rushed in. Muria was pacing up and down.

"Something very bad is going on in the mountains," she said, "The Green Lord came into the clearing half an hour back and asked for our help to prevent it getting any worse. You can imagine how serious this is if he came himself rather than sending animals or lesser fairies to alert us. And, indeed, if he came in broad daylight on a day which is not a festival."

"What's happening?" asked Yssa.

"You remember the message from the rabbits and moles a few days ago? I sent word immediately to Lord Therron and he dispatched a party of men to investigate. But the Green Lord says that they are heading for Lord Yevon's castle while the danger lies elsewhere. It seems Lord Yevon has been using explosives underground, and is planning to use an even bigger charge very soon in the mountains some way from the castle. The fairies have tried to lead Lord Therron's men in the right direction, but there is nobody in the party who can hear fairy speech. The Green Lord wants all of us - all the half-fays - to go as quickly as possible to act as interpreters."

"How will we know where Lord Therron's men are? How will we catch up with them?" asked Milon.

"The Green Lord is sending fairies to guide us by the shortest route. I have sent an even more urgent message to Lord Therron asking for horses and grooms. It's the only way we can hope to reach the others in time and I can't get a message to Liana in time, so we five will have to suffice. Now, while I wait for an answer, you'd better go to Cassie and ask her to find you clothes for riding. Hurry now, and come back here as fast as you can."

By the time the quartet returned wearing breeches and jerkins, as Tiera had done for the journey to Lord Felsal's, a guard in Lord Therron's uniform had arrived with his master's reply. Muria untied the scroll and read:

"I am organising men and horses even as I write. Meet them at the main gateway into the forest within the hour. I thank you, as always, for liaising between ourselves and the Forest Beings. In haste, Therron."

"It will take us half an hour to walk to the main gateway," said Muria, "We have no time to lose. Now, I had better go to Cassie and get some breeches, too!"

She was on her way out of the door when she almost collided with Ruid on his way in.

"What's going on?" he asked abruptly, "I just saw Cassie and she said she'd been fitting people up with riding gear. Has Lord Felsal asked for help again?"

"No, the Green Lord has," and Muria rapidly filled him in on what was happening."

"Then I'm coming with you," declared Ruid.

"We can't both leave the Hall at the same time," replied Muria.

Tama and Allya can cope, they'll have to, and Cassie's always there if they need an older person to refer to."

"I say no."

"And I say yes!"

It was the nearest any of the young people had ever seen to a quarrel between their teachers, and the two appeared still to be arguing fiercely as they headed off in the direction of the Sanctuary. But they were both wearing riding gear when they came back.

****

At the forest gate men and horses were assembled, harnesses jingling. To the Dancers' surprise, Lord Therron sat astride the leading horse. Leaning down, he grasped Muria's hand and said,

"Your message sounded so grave that I felt I must

lead this group myself. We have the fastest horses from my stables, spare mounts and the most experienced riders so if your party are ready, we will be off. Lead the way."

Six men stepped forward to help the Dancers into the saddle. Milon felt undignified riding in front of a burly guard, just as the girls were doing, but it was no time to bother about one's pride. Then they were off.

As soon as the party was through the gate, an elf appeared from between the trees and said,

"Follow the main track to the first fork, then take the left branch." Muria conveyed this to Lord Therron and they set off at a gallop along the broad track. At the fork, another elf was waiting for them.

"Take the right branch next time the track divides," he said, and they rode on without slowing and at each fork in the track another elf would be waiting to give them directions. Dusk came as they rode deeper into the Forest, but as the dusk deepened and night fell, fireflies and glow worms appeared all round them, marking the edge of the track and giving them enough light to avoid any obstacles.

At the next fork, the Green Lord himself awaited them, mounted on a mighty stag with seven-branched antlers.

"I will ride with you to the edge of the Forest," he said, guiding his stag onto the path.

Tiera gazed at him in awe. This was the first time she had seen him so clearly and so close, for on all the occasions when he had appeared among the Dancers he had sparkled in and out of vision.

She studied his noble face, his deep green eyes, his beard of oak-leaves and his green oak-leaf hair. Then he turned and smiled. It seemed to Tiera that he was looking straight at her, and she looked away, embarrassed to have been caught staring.

For the next hour the Dancers followed the stag and Lord Therron and his guards followed the Dancers. Tiera had to remind herself several times that nobody except the half-fays could see the Green Lord and his mighty stag. Lord Therron, of course, knew what was happening and trusted Muria and the other Dancers implicitly, but she wondered whether his men knew that they were being led by the Lord of the fairies.

At each fork in the track, the way got narrower and before long they were strung out in single file. Branches overhung the path, and the riders had often to duck to avoid being struck about the head and their progress slowed. At the back of the column rode a group of guards each with a second, riderless horse on a leading rein, and it required a great deal of manoeuvring to keep them from getting tangled in the bushes.

On through the night they rode until they saw that the trees were thinning out a little.

"Soon we will be at the edge of the Forest," said the Green Lord, "and I can come no further with you but the dwarves will be waiting to guide you the rest of the way."

Before they reached the Forest margin, though, they passed though an area where not a single tree remained.

"This is where all the trouble started," the Green Lord said, "Where Yevon began felling trees. Noble oaks and elms stood here, all kinds of bushes grew beneath them, and mosses and grasses below that. The creatures who lived here have lost their homes and it will take hundreds of years to replace. Now we know his purpose, and we must stop him, we *will* stop him before he does even more harm."

"Lord Therron established that he had felled trees to make pit props, and the rabbits and moles talked of men making burrows," Muria asked him, "Do you know why?"

"Yes, the Lady Khoda, Yevon's wife, wants an amethyst to rival the Great Geode. She thinks it will give her power. He has had men digging for months in the hope of finding one and as they have not succeeded he intends to use gunpowder. We have to stop him before he does that."

Now they could dimly see open country ahead, and several tiny men waiting beside the track. The Green Lord dismounted from his stag and the Dancers followed suit. Seeing them, the dwarves came towards the forest path.

"Now I am going to hand you over to the mountain dwellers, who will guide you the rest of the way. Good speed to you, and may your mission succeed," said the Green Lord, remounting the great stag and disappearing into the forest.

"I am Ord and this is Gotti, this is Nedo and this is Druk," said the tiny man who seemed to be the dwarves' leader. He was about as tall as a six-year old child, but clearly far greater than that in age, for he had a long grey beard, and the wisps of hair that showed beneath his dull yellow cap were grey too. Apart from the cap and a dusty green jacket, his clothes were also grey and so were his high boots. His companions were similarly dressed and, apart from Nedo who was beardless and had brown hair, looked just as ancient.

"Your party will have to split in two now," said Ord, "We need to send some of Lord Therron's men to divert the other group, while the rest of us hurry on towards the mines. Two of us will go with them, and we'll need two of the half-fays to interpret."

"Why two of us?" queried Muria.

"They may need to send somebody back with messages," said Ord.

Muria conveyed this information to Lord Therron,

who decided rapidly to send the most senior of the guards to intercept his original party.

"If I send Captain Kado they'll take orders from him," he explained, "Now which of your group will ride with him to interpret for the dwarves?"

It was quickly settled that Yssa and Milon should go with the Captain, and Lord Therron called for fresh horses for them. All the horses that had been on leading reins were brought forward now, Captain Kado transferred his bags from his original mount, and they set off with Nedo and Gotti running alongside. For all their tiny size, they seemed to keep pace effortlessly with the horses. Ord, seeing the look of astonishment on Tiera's face, laughed and said,

"They've got their seven-league boots on today!"

Lord Therron was organising the transfer of riders and bags from their tired horses to the fresh ones and as soon as that had been accomplished they were ready to set off, following the remaining dwarves. They must have seven-league boots, too, Tiera thought, seeing how fast they ran. But before long, they all had to slow down, for the way was becoming steeper. At least it was getting light now, and they could see where to guide the horses. The ground looked dry and barren, and again and again they saw deep cracks in the ground.

"You see that?" asked Ord, "Yevon's had men tunnelling under here without enough supports, and the ground is caving in. And there's worse ahead, I promise you."

Indeed, as the horses picked their way higher up the hillside, the cracks grew deeper and more numerous and Tiera could see that much of the ground was covered with stones and rubble, burying any plants that might once have grown there.

"These used to be fertile meadows, full of flowers, rich grazing for the cows in summer and home to more small animals and insects than you can imagine," said Ord. "They were full of beautiful flowers and rare herbs that people use as medicines. Now Yevon has covered them with all the rock hauled out of the tunnels his men have been making."

They struggled on upwards for a little longer, until suddenly Ord cried,

"Ah, I see Wilkin waiting for us. He's the miner who first alerted us to what Yevon is up to."

Sitting on a large boulder was a grey-haired man, not much bigger than Ord himself, who jumped up waving both arms at them as they approached.

"Thank goodness!" he shouted, "I wondered if you were ever going to get here. Come on, we've no time to lose. His Lordship's planning to blast open the Great Chamber today. He's already down there somewhere. We've got to stop him."

CHAPTER SIXTEEN

They stood on the barren mountainside: dwarves, half-fays and men. They'd tethered the horses some way downhill, when it became too steep for them to climb any further. Wilkin the miner began to explain the situation.

"Yevon and his mad wife are somewhere under here with a large quantity of gunpowder, and not the foggiest idea how to use it safely. If we don't reach them before they try to light it, they could blow out the whole hillside."

At this, even the toughest of Lord Therron's men gasped.

"Obviously, the most urgent thing is to get a party down there, enough men to hold them back by force," Wilkin continued, "Then we need to set guards at the entrances to all the tunnels in case they try to escape - that is, if they don't blow themselves to smithereens first! There are four tunnels which all lead to the Great Chamber. We'll need four men at each entrance, enough to restrain two people trying to escape."

"We could do with more men," said Lord Therron, "I wish I knew how long it might take for the other detachment to reach us."

"We'll just have to manage with those we have," said Wilkin.

Then Ord stepped forward and said,

"We'll need a half-fay to go with the main party to translate for the dwarves who are waiting to guide you through the tunnels, and others to do the same at the tunnel-mouths."

"That's five," said Muria, "There are only three of us here. The other two went with Gotti and Nedo."

"Then I'll go with the main party," said Wilkin, "I understand dwarvish, but it still leaves us one short."

Just then, they saw two figures struggling up the steep path below them.

"It's Milon!" cried Tiera, "Just in time. I guess that's one of the guards with him."

Lord Therron set off at a run to meet them. From above, Tiera watched as he reached them, conversed briefly and sent the guard back downhill. Milon and

Lord Therron scrambled uphill as fast as the steep incline and loose rocks would allow.

"Thank goodness," said Lord Therron, "the rest of the men aren't too far off. Milon and Brudo came on ahead to let us know. I've sent Brudo back to guide them, but we have Milon now to make up the complement of half-fays." He was already moving among his men, organising them into five groups. He turned to Wilkin and said,

"The best we can do for now is leave two men at each tunnel entrance, with one half-fay, and orders for two more from the second troop to join them as soon as they get here. It seems more important at this moment to get a party moving towards where you think Yevon is headed."

"I agree," said Wilkin.

"Absolutely," said Ord.

"You lead, and I'll follow you with some of my men," said Lord Therron, "Though I wish there were more of them."

"I'm coming with you," said Ruid.

"Good man! Numbers may be vital," said Lord

Therron as he followed Ord and Wilkin towards a low hole in the mountainside. One by one they bent double and disappeared inside.

Druk gathered the remaining men and half-fays together and pointed out the other entrances, one of them some way downhill, the other two further down. They spread out and waited for reinforcements.

****

In the tunnel, Wilkin led the way. It was pitch black, except for a feeble light from a lantern that he carried, and the men stumbled forwards, bent double, often bumping against the sides of the narrow shaft. Ord brought up the rear with another lantern. The tunnel began to slope sharply downwards, and from time to time they had to climb over piles of fallen rock.

"That's where the ceiling has caved in because he didn't use enough pit props," said Wilkin, "I told him. He didn't listen."

It didn't exactly inspire confidence! But they pressed on, crawling now, past any number of side tunnels. Whenever they passed a junction, there was a dwarf waiting.

"This tunnel's a dead end. Keep going. Yevon hasn't been this way today, but we have heard voices echoing," said the first one to Wilkin, who passed the news on to the others.

They crawled on. At the next junction, the dwarf had similar information, and so on until they came to a small natural chamber where three tunnels met. The ceiling here was higher and it was a relief to the humans in the party to be able to stand almost upright. Here, several dwarves were waiting, and the news they had was not good.

"Yevon came through here not long since," said one, "with the woman, and two other men carrying bundles. They came from the top tunnel."

Wilkin and Lord Therron conferred:

"This is not good," said Lord Therron, keeping his voice low. He did not want it to echo in the tunnels and reveal their presence. "If there are four people ahead of us, we may be too few to overpower them."

"Why don't I go back to the surface and see if the

rest of the men have arrived?" suggested Ord, "I can move through the shafts a lot faster than any of you."

"Yes. Go as fast as you can!"

The rest squatted down in the half-dark to wait. They could hear stones scattering as Ord hurried back towards the surface, then there was an uncanny silence. Suddenly, it was broken by a female voice echoing clearly in the tunnels.

"Idiot...iot...iot....iot.....ot.......ot.."

Wilkin suppressed the urge to laugh, though it was no laughing matter.

"It's her, the Lady Khoda," he whispered. "It's always been thought bad luck for a woman to enter the mines, but that one's bad luck wherever she is. All of this is due to her."

They sat in silence again, until they heard the wonderful, welcome sound of reinforcements scraping their way through the shaft behind them. As they emerged into the chamber, Ruid saw that Milon was immediately behind Druk.

"Milon!" whispered Ruid, "Why have you come down here? I thought you were minding one of the

227

entrances?"

"Yssa's there now. I came in case I was needed to translate between Druk and the men."

There was no arguing with this but Ruid said,

"Keep towards the back of the line, Milon. Let Lord Therron's men go ahead."

And now that they had a good number of men, it was time to move forward.

****

On the hillside, Tiera crouched next to the tunnel-mouth, four burly guards alongside her. She could see Yssa with the guards at entrance above her, Muria at the one below and Lyria at the lowest. It seemed a terribly long time since Lord Therron and the first party had gone into the tunnels, and now Milon had gone after them with more men.

She bit her fingers. Anything could happen to them under the ground: Ruid who she had worshipped since the day he'd scooped her out of a bush in the Sacred

Forest, and Milon who she had grown more and more fond of since the summer. It was only now that he may be in danger that she realised just *how* fond. But there was nothing she could do except wait.

The morning wore on. Sometimes she thought she could hear voices echoing from the tunnel; other times she thought she was imagining them.

"Cheer up lass!" said one of the guards, and she tried her best to smile.

Suddenly, there was a rumbling like thunder below her feet. The guards were instantly alert. Then came a deafening explosion. Downhill from where they stood, rocks flew into the air, followed by an avalanche of smaller stones.

"Milon! Ruid!" Tiera screamed, and heard Yssa's voice echoing hers downhill. Birds flew into the air cawing, hooting, shrieking.

Then there was absolute silence. Not even the sound of a stone rolling downhill.

"What can we do? What can we do? They might be hurt," Tiera cried, but the eldest of the guards with her said,

"Stay put, lass, there's nothing you can do down there."

After an eternity, it seemed, Druk emerged like a bolt from the tunnel-mouth. Tiera grabbed his shoulders,

"Is everyone alright? Is anybody hurt? What happened?"

"The idiots set off the charge before we could stop them. They may be dead, for all I know, but it brought down some rock in the tunnel and one or two of the men are trapped."

"Who? Who? Do you know who?"

"No. The others are digging rock away from them. We'll know in a little while."

Tears ran down Tiera's face. Ruid, Milon, either of them could be hurt. Or both of them. They could be dead. 'Trapped' could mean crushed to death under rocks, she thought. Then a slim figure crawled out of the opening. His face was so blackened it took her a moment to realise who it was.

"Milon! It's you. You're alive. You're not hurt," she

screamed, flinging herself at him and sobbing with relief.

"No, but Ruid is," he replied, hugging her hard enough to hurt, "He's unconscious, hit on the head by a rock, and his legs are trapped. The men are digging him out now. I came out to see if there is anything we could use as a stretcher."

They scanned the hillside for anything that might serve, but there was nothing remotely likely. Only stone.

"A travelling cloak, then, we could wrap that round him and drag him out. It's the only way. The tunnel's too low for two men to carry him."

One of the guards was already half-running, half-sliding down the hill toward the tethered horses. Yssa, recognising her brother, was scrambling uphill to throw her arms round him, sobbing like Tiera. Muria and Lyria had left their posts and were climbing up towards them as fast as they could.

Before they could reach the main entrance, the guard had got back carrying a long cloak. Milon took it from him and turned to go back down the tunnel.

"Don't go, don't go," cried Tiera.

"I must," Milon said, disentangling himself from Tiera and his sister, and disappeared into the tunnel-mouth.

Now Muria and Lyria reached them and seeing Yssa and Tiera both weeping, asked anxiously,

"What's happened?"

"Ruid's hurt. He's unconscious. His legs are trapped. The men are trying to dig him out," the girls sobbed between them.

Muria's face registered the shock that all of them were feeling, but she said at once,

"We must work a healing for him. Now. Dancing is impossible here, but we can use the hand movements and focus our minds on Ruid."

To the astonishment of the guards, the four of them knelt down on the stones and began to hum a tune, moving their hands rhythmically as they did so slowly at first, then faster and faster until they finally slowed right down and stopped. After that, there was nothing they could do except wait.

After what seemed like a terribly long time, Druk

the dwarf appeared again and said,

"It looks as if your chap is going to be alright. He's regained consciousness, and they're bringing him out now."

****

Castle Yevon had never seen such a motley array of people, at least, never in living memory. Young and old, men and women, lords and miners, guards and dancers, humans and dwarves, they were all standing, sitting or lying in the great hall. Somewhere below, in the dungeons, the castle's owner and his wife were in chains, watched over by men from Lord Therron's guard. Therron had decided the best thing to do with the two injured men was to get them indoors as quickly as possible, and Castle Yevon was the nearest habitation to the hillside where so much drama had enfolded earlier in the day.

Besides the two casualties - and he knew they were very lucky that there were no more - he was conscious that none of his men, nor the Dancers had slept or eaten since the previous day. To have attempted to ride back to Allegria once he had got everybody out of the mines would have been madness. So, once the injured men had been carried down the mountainside to the horses, he had ordered improvised hammocks to be slung between two pairs of horses to carry them to the castle. Ruid, though still weak, insisted that he was fit enough to ride, but Lord Therron signalled to his men to leave the second hammock in place, as two of his men carried a heavy bundle downhill from the tunnels. This they heaved into position between the two horses, and the column set off.

As soon as they reached the castle, Lord Therron sent men to explore the place and it was not long before they had discovered most of Lord Yevon's servants hiding in larders, alcoves, any nook or cranny where they thought they might escape notice. Once they realised that the men served Lord Therron, ruler of all Kerran, and meant them no harm they crept out, willing to do his bidding.

So, he had ordered nourishing food to be produced as quickly as possible, hot water to wash wounds, and a great deal more hot water later for bathing. He had stable-men attending to the horses and chamber maids making up every bed in the castle, and because he was a merciful ruler, he even made sure that food was taken down to the dungeons.

Now that everybody had eaten and Ruid and the guard Jenk had been made comfortable, they gathered in the great hall to piece together the events of the day. The dwarves were nervous, unused to being inside human habitations, and they clustered round Wilkin with whom they felt more at home. Tiera, sitting between Muria and Lyria on a low couch, struggled to keep her eyes open, but was determined to stay awake until she had heard the whole story. Milon, his clothes ripped and his face still black, sat opposite with his sister. Catching his eye, Tiera blushed. It was not until she'd feared he might be dead that she had realised just how much Milon meant to her, and his fierce hug when he emerged from the mine suggested he felt the same. But now Lord Therron was speaking.

"Wilkin, let's hear from you first," he said, "Without you, Yevon might have got away with this

235

dreadful business."

CHAPTER SEVENTEEN

"Well, my lord, the first I knew about all this was when Lord Yevon sent his man, Quar, to fetch me up here. He wanted me to find a giant geode for her Ladyship, except that the name "Lady" is too good for her, if you'll pardon me saying so. I found out later that he'd already tried to steal the Great Geode from the temple to keep her happy."

Lord Therron's eyebrows nearly disappeared into his hair and there was muttering and murmuring all around. This was the first they had heard of that.

"He didn't succeed, of course. So he sent for me and ordered me to find one as big, if not bigger. I told him there was not a chance. Nothing that big has ever been found since the Great Chamber was shut off by a rock fall, and that was over a hundred years ago. So he ordered me to get the Great Chamber opened up."

At this point, the dwarf, Ord, reached up and whispered something in Wilkin's ear.

"Ord reminds me, my lord, to point out that after the

rock fall, both men and dwarves agreed never to reopen that cave. In those days, they cooperated a lot more than now."

"The dwarves have certainly cooperated with us," said Lord Therron, "I don't like to think what might have happened without their help. But go on."

"Well, I didn't like the idea one little bit, but I could hardly say no. Yevon is the Lord of this Province, he owns the cabin I live in, he owns the whole village, so I started tunnelling, in the hope we might find something to keep her Ladyship happy without doing any great harm. But he hired inexperienced men, didn't give us enough timber for props, and when it was clear we were never to going to find anything really big, he decided to use explosives. Or rather, she did. That's when I said I'd have nothing more to do with it. My family have always cut crystals by hand. We've done so for hundreds of years. That way, nothing is damaged."

"It was an ancestor of yours who found the Great Geode, I believe," said Lord Therron.

"Yes, my Lord, with help from the dwarves," Wilkin replied. "As I said before, we worked together in those days. My family respects the Earth, just as the dwarves do. But, to get back to what's just happened: when I found out they had got enough gunpowder to blast open the Great Chamber - don't ask me how - I sent my son off to Allegria to alert you. Finally, I realised it was imminent, and that my son wouldn't reach you in time, so I asked Ord here to get a message to you. The rest you know."

"Wilkin, we owe you more thanks than I can ever express. You shall be rewarded."

"I don't ask for any reward, my lord, I'm just happy to have helped prevent more damage than Yevon has caused already. But I think the people who weren't actually in the mine, the ladies particularly, want to hear what happened down there."

"Indeed," said Lord Therron, "But there is not a great deal to tell. There's a maze of passage under the ground, some very old, some recently excavated, and it is thanks to Ord and Druk and their friends that we found our way towards the Great Chamber without getting lost."

"Three cheers for the dwarves!" came a voice from

the back of the hall, and everybody joined in the cheering with a will. When the echoes had died away, Lord Therron went on.

"We hoped to reach Lord Yevon and his wife before they could do any harm, but they must have heard us approaching - the tiniest sound echoes in those tunnels - and were about to light the fuse when we reached them. Yevon had a lit taper in his hand. I knocked it out of his hand, and was about to stamp on it when his wife seized it and screamed 'I'll kill you! I'll kill all of you, even if I die too!' and flung it at the fuse. You all heard the blast, of course. You can imagine how it sounded in the tunnels. We were all knocked back by the blast and blackened by soot and, as you know, Ruid and Jenk were trapped by falling rock. The miracle, though, is that only a small portion of the gunpowder ignited. When we crawled through the rubble to investigate afterwards, we found a good three quarters of it still there. It seems the fuse had not reached that far.

"Amateurs!" said Wilkin.

" If it had all caught, I should not be here to speak to you now, nor would any of the brave men who were

240

with us in the mine."

Tiera began to silently weep again, at the thought of Milon and Ruid lying dead underground.

"And what about Lord Yevon and his wife?" asked Lyria.

"They were blasted straight into our arms!" laughed Lord Therron, "Them and the two men they had with them, blackened and deafened by the blast, but otherwise unharmed."

"Pity!" one of the guards said.

"No, it is not a pity," Lord Therron reproved him gently. "It is better that they live and come to trial. Now, none of us has slept since yesterday, so I think it's time we found beds for everybody. And, once again, I thank every single person who's been involved in this. The damage Lord Yevon has caused will take a very long time to undo, but today an entire hillside might have been blasted away without your help. And now, good night!"

****

Tiera woke with a start in a strange bed in a strange room. The sun was high, so she knew she had slept late. Then it all came flooding back: the dramas and fears of yesterday, the journey through the forest the night before. No wonder she had slept so long! She look around and saw Lyria asleep in a bed next to hers. They were in what was obviously a servants' room high in one of the towers. There was another bed, empty now, that had clearly been slept in. She remembered now: Yssa had been in that bed. She slid out of bed, carefully so as not to wake Lyria, and got dressed. She was reluctant to put on her clothes from the day before, filthy now, but she had no alternative. Leaving Lyria sleeping, she made her way down the winding stairs in search of other people and of food. She got lost in the maze of stairs and corridors, but finally heard voices and followed them until she came to the great hall.

Muria was there, talking to Lord Therron.

"Good morning, young Tiera," he smiled.

"Have you had breakfast?" Muria asked, "No? Then why don't you go down to the kitchen and see what they can find for you - it's that way, down those stairs.

Then come back to me here, we're going to make a healing dance for Ruid and then another for Jenk."

"Thank you. I'll be as quick as I can," said Tiera.

"Don't hurry. Eat what you need, and come to us later."

Tiera had only been in the kitchen a few minutes, and was sitting at a table with a glass of milk and some cornbread, when Lyria came down the steps, rubbing her eyes. She'd found her way straight from the bedroom to the kitchen without getting lost en route! While they ate, Tiera told her that they were expected in the great hall when they'd eaten, to make healing dances for Ruid and Jenk, and as soon as they had both finished and thanked the cook, they ran upstairs to the hall. All the Dancers were there now, and somebody had made a space around one of the couches. Muria surveyed her Dancers in their torn and dirty clothes and burst out laughing.

"This is a very far cry from the Sanctuary and our purple robes!" she laughed, "but we must look beyond the surface and focus our healing thoughts on Ruid and Jenk. As Ruid is here already, let us start with him."

Lord Therron said, "I'll leave you, and give orders that you are not be disturbed. Let me know when you are ready for Jenk and I'll have two men carry him in. Both his legs are broken, you know."

"Your legs were broken, too," said Muria to Ruid after Lord Therron had gone, "We picked that up when we scanned you."

"I had no idea. I was unconscious. I guess they began to knit when you worked a healing for me, but I'll be grateful to receive a full dance today as well. I feel weak and it's true that my shins still hurt."

"We'd have made a healing for Jenk then if we could, but we didn't know who else was hurt apart from yourself," said Muria, "Now, lie down and we'll begin."

Milon held Ruid's feet, Muria, as ever was at his head, and Tiera and Yssa stood either side of him. Lyria's role was to sing the music, though they all joined in. Tiera was deeply moved to be taking part in a healing for Ruid, dear Ruid who had been like an uncle to her. No, not even an uncle, more like the father she never knew.

When they had done, they crept out of the hall leaving Ruid to sleep for a little while. Muria went in search of Lord Therron so that he could arrange for Jenk to be brought into the hall, and the younger Dancers went out into the courtyard in search of sunshine and some fresh air, for much of the castle smelt stale and fusty.

After a while, Ruid came out to join them, smiling and hugged each one of them in turn.

"My thanks to all of you," he said, "I feel well enough to teach three or four dance classes non-stop!"

They all laughed, but were truly happy to see their teacher restored to his usual self. Why, any minute he might start cracking one of his atrocious jokes! Now one of Lord Therron's men came to tell them that Jenk was ready for them, and they followed him back into the hall.

This time, Tiera changed places with Lyria, then once again, they set about their healing work. Jenk, unused to such things, looked very nervous at first, but Muria put him at his ease, and then they began the dance. As usual, at the end, they stole away leaving him in silence. Muria went in search of Lord Therron, to ask if there was anybody else hurt.

"No, only cuts and bruises that will heal without help, and now it's time to think about getting back to Allegria. I shall call Captains Kado and Brudo and get the men and horses organised, then we should be away as soon as we can."

****

It was a strange troop that rode into Allegria, so strange that people stopped in the streets to stare. Kerran is a peaceful country, and it was very unusual to see Lord Therron's guards in anything but ceremonial uniforms, guarding his residence. But here was Lord Therron himself, in torn and filthy clothes, at the head of a column of equally tattered men. In the middle of the column came Lord Yevon and his wife; not that most citizens of Allegria knew who they were. Their hands were tied behind them and they were seated backwards, facing their horses' rumps - a position of the utmost humiliation. Behind them came Quar the steward and

Rhodi, Lady Khoda's footman, similarly trussed. Behind them again rode half a dozen Dancers, who many of the bystanders recognised, though they too wore torn and dirty clothes, then a very small, grey haired man, watching like a hawk over two horses that had some heavy burden slung between them, and finally more of Lord Therron's tattered men.

They rode through the main streets, clearly in high spirits despite their tatterdemalion appearance, and turned in to the courtyard of Lord Therron's palace.

Lord Therron jumped down from his mount and ran to Muria.

"Don't dismount," he said, "It would be unthinkable to make you walk the last lap home! The men will ride to Dancers' Hall with you then bring the horses back here."

He took Muria's hand in his and kissed it gallantly.

"I will contact you in a day or two, when you have had time to recover from all your exertions," he said.

****

The trial of Lord Yevon and Lady Khoda was held in the great main square of Allegria. Lord Therron had decided that it should be as public as possible, so that every citizen might learn that harming the Sacred Forest and the ancient hills would never be tolerated in Kerran. He had a platform constructed with banks of seats facing it, but even they were not enough to hold all who wanted to hear the trial, and many more stood around the square each day.

On the platform Lord Therron sat with the chief Justiciars and the Lords of each of Kerran's provinces, who he had called to sit in judgement with him. There was Lord Lars from Madran in the south, Lord Radnel from the western province of Torven, Lord Felsal from Illia, and the Lady Fendra, who governed Maritima.

Wilkin the miner was the chief witness, then came servants from Castle Yevon, men who had been pressed against their will into tunnelling, farmers who had lost their pastures, woodsmen who described the desecration of the forest. Tiera, Milon, Yssa and Lyria told how the animals had brought them messages, Muria read out a message from the Green Lord himself.

Then Lord Yevon and the Lady Khoda were questioned. Lord Yevon trembled and muttered,

"I only wanted to keep my wife happy. Besides, the mines were under my lands, surely I could do what I liked with them?"

"Not when that meant turning a fertile hillside into a barren waste," said Lord Therron.

The Lady Khoda, though, was defiant.

"Just because you have the biggest amethyst in all Kerran here in Allegria, you think you have power over everybody else. If I'd got my hands on one I'd have taught you a few lessons!" she sneered.

"The Great Geode has nothing to do with power. It's purpose is healing," said Lord Therron.

The questioning went on for several days, Quar the steward and Rhodi the footman were questioned closely about their part in the matter. Quar continually tried to justify his actions, but the more he did so the more he tied himself in knots. Rhodi the footman was so nervous he could hardly speak, but it soon became clear that he had been ordered by Lady Khoda to carry a bundle into the mine, and had had no idea what was in it.

Then the Justiciars and Lords went away to consider their verdict.

On the final day, the square was packed with people. There was a great hush as Lord Therron and the regional governors filed onto the platform, followed by the Justiciars and a good many scribes. Finally came the guards escorting the four prisoners.

Lord Therron stood up and in a loud voice began to speak.

"Citizens of Allegria, citizens of Kerran, I have conferred with the chief Justiciars of this land and all the Governors, and we are agreed on the following: That Citizens Yevon and Khoda are guilty of desecrating the Sacred Forest and the mountains of Swathia and that Citizen Yevon is also guilty of attempting to steal the Great Geode from the temple. According to the ancient statutes of Kerran both these crimes carry the death penalty."

A murmur of shock ran round the square. Lord Therron waited for calm before he went on,

"But we live in more enlightened times, so we have

determined that they should be stripped of their titles and exiled from Kerran."

Another ripple went through the crowd.

"As for the steward Quar, it is clear that he was complicit in these crimes from beginning to end, and we sentence him to ten years' imprisonment. Finally, we pardon the footman Rhodi, who was clearly dragged into this at the last moment and against his will."

There was some cheering, a great buzz of talk, and over it all Citizen Khoda could be heard screaming curses at everybody in sight. Not that it availed her at all: the guards were leading her and her husband back to the city jail to await the ship that would carry them away from Kerran for ever.

CHAPTER EIGHTEEN

The day after the trial ended, Muria received an invitation from Lord Therron to attend a banquet at his palace, bringing Ruid, Tiera, Milon, Yssa and Lyria with her. There was much excitement and discussion of what to wear. Cassie, when consulted, decided on the white robes and tunics from the last Midsummer rites.

"I can always wash them if you spill your dinner down the front!" she chuckled.

At the palace they were ushered into the same hall where Lord Therron had pronounced on Tiera's future, but now it was laid out with long tables and garlands of flowers were festooned all round the walls. Servants bustled in and out with huge dishes as Lord Therron came forward to greet them.

"Welcome, my dear Dancers," he said, as he led them to seats near the top end of the main table, "Everybody involved in the downfall of Yevon is here tonight. This is my way of thanking you."

Lord Therron and Lady Helma sat at the head of the

table with Wilkin at Lady Helma's right hand and Muria at Lord Therron's left. Next to Wilkin sat the Lady Bethna, then her husband, Lord Felsal and Tiera was happy to find that she was placed next to him and even more delighted that Milon sat to her right. Opposite them sat Muria next to Lord Lars with his Lady Nassia then Ruid, Yssa, Lord Radnel and so on, Dancers alternating with the Lords and Ladies. Further down the table she could see red-robed Justiciars, scribes, Captain Kado, Captain Brudo, Jenk and other guards she recognised.

Tiera was almost too nervous to eat at first, but relaxed when she realised that nobody was standing on ceremony, but were all taking freely and informally among themselves. From Lord Felsal she learnt that Ildon was now a sturdy little boy and they reminisced about the Dancers' visit to Illia. Lord Lars, across the table listened intently and wanted to know more, which Muria was more than happy to tell him. At one point, Tiera overheard Muria saying to Wilkin,

"You talk with the dwarves. Are you a half-blood too?"

"Ah no, not me, but I reckon I do have a smidgin of dwarf blood in my veins from way back. It may have been my great-great-grandfather, or my great-great-great-grandfather who took a dwarf girl to bride, I don't know, but my family's always been able to understand dwarvish and, as you can see, we tend to be on the small side."

And so the meal went on, course after delicious course, until the servants were clearing away the dessert dishes and Lord Therron stood up and clapped his hands for attention.

"Good friends, I invited you all here tonight for a number of reasons: one, to say thank you to everybody present, secondly to announce the name of the new governor of Swathia, thirdly .... well, we'll come to that later!"

All eyes were on him, and there was absolute silence as everyone waited to hear who was to succeed Yevon as Lord of Swathia.

"I have conferred with all the regional Governors, and they all agree with me that the new governor of Swathia should be......... Lord Wilkin!"

Wilkin turned white, then blushed red as Lord Therron hauled him to his feet, and everybody stood and cheered.

"A toast to Lord Wilkin!" cried Lord Therron, and there were more cheers as people raised their goblets.

"Speech! Speech!"

Wilkin blushed an even deeper red and stammered,

"My Lord, Lords, Ladies, everybody....No, it's not right. I'm just a miner, my family have been miners for generations. I mean, we aren't grand or noble or anything......"

"You acted with far greater nobility than one of my supposed nobles," interrupted Lord Therron, "You proved that you love the mountains of Swathia and we are confident that you are the right person to care for them in future and oversee the great task of restoration."

Wilkin was too choked with emotion to say any more and sat down, brushing tears from his eyes. But Lord Therron pulled him to his feet again and led him to the rostrum at the end of the hall, on which stood a mysterious object, covered by a velvet cloth.

"I mentioned a third reason why I called you all together tonight," said Lord Therron "and I think it is right that Lord Wilkin should reveal it to us all."

At a signal from Lord Therron, Wilkin pulled nervously at a corner of the cloth, then a little harder. As the cloth fell away, there was an astonished silence, then gasps and cheers as people abandoned the tables and pressed forward for a better view of a very large, brilliant amethyst geode.

"Tell them what happened, Wilkin," Lord Therron said, putting his arm round the new Lord's shoulder.

"Er, well, you see.... oh dear, I don't think I'll ever get used to this... you see, after the explosion, when we tried to clear away the rubble, this is what we found."

"I should explain," said Lord Therron, "that it did not look at all like it does now. It looked like a rather boring lump of rock! If it were not for the expertise of Lord Wilkin nobody would have had any idea what it was."

"Well, I've mined a good few geodes in my time, though none as big as this," said Lord Wilkin, "so I know what to look for. I reckoned once it had been cut and cleaned up a bit it wouldn't look too bad!"

At this, everybody burst out laughing. 'Not too bad' totally failed to describe the beauty and magnificence of the stone. It was quite a lot smaller than the Great Geode itself, but every bit as beautiful.

"I do not know what it's eventual use will be," said Lord Therron, "But I am sure that will become clear when the time is right."

Now servants were carrying away the last of the dishes and removing the long trestles. Some of the guests took their leave of Lord Therron and Lady Helma, and the rest chattered in little knots here and there. Tiera saw that Lord Felsal and Lady Bethna were talking earnestly with Muria, and after a few moments she beckoned the other Dancers to join them.

"Lord Felsal wants to know if we have come to any decision about setting up a second Dancers' Hall in Illia," she said, "and I'm afraid I had to tell him that we have had other preoccupations lately!"

Lord Felsal laughed. "That I understand only too well," he said, "but while my good Lady and I are in Allegria it would be a good time to talk about it some more."

Lord Therron came and joined their group and, hearing the topic of conversation, said,

"Felsal and I have talked about this a little. I think it is an excellent idea. In fact, I think perhaps there should be a Dancers' Hall in each of the provinces, but of course it is for the Dancers to decide."

"It grows late," said Muria, "and I should get my young people home to bed. Lord Felsal, suppose you and the Lady Bethna visit Dancers' Hall tomorrow so that we can discuss this in more detail?"

****

Muria and Ruid, Tama and Allya gathered in Muria's study a long time before Lord Felsal and his wife were expected. Although Tama and Ruid had mentioned the idea as soon as they got back from their visit to Illia, the business of Lord Yevon and the mine had intervened immediately, and this was the first time they had all sat down together to give it serious thought. Ruid outlined once again what Lord Felsal had suggested and what his reply had been.

"Certainly it couldn't be done in a hurry, if at all," said Allya, who had not been present on that earlier occasion.

"But do you think it is worth considering, or should we reject the idea out of hand?" asked Muria.

"I think we should at least consider it," said Tama, "It was clear when we were there that there is a real need."

"How could it be done?" asked Allya, "It would need a good number of dancers. Could we spare that many?"

"Let's think what is the minimum number of people that would be needed to set up a new Hall," suggested Ruid.

"Well, for a start," said Muria, "A new Hall would need at least one senior teacher and enough people to perform healing dances, including at least one half-fay, but that would not be enough for the big Festivals, the Solstices and Equinoxes, and any other days that are special festivals in individual provinces."

"If there was a handful of fully trained dancers,"

mused Tama, "most of the Dancers at the Festivals could be students, as they are here. But obviously local children would need to be trained as soon as possible to build up the numbers."

And so they went on, until Lord Felsal and Lady Bethna were due. To everyone's surprise, Lord Therron came with them.

"This is a matter that concerns the whole of Kerran," he said, explaining his presence. "I feel that if you establish a second Dancers' Hall in Illia, there would be a good case for doing the same in the other provinces. So, I hope you will permit me to join in your discussions."

A long time later, the whole group emerged from Muria's study onto the lawn, smiling.

"Well," said Lord Therron, "That is agreed. Lord Felsal will start on the construction of a new Hall which will take some time, and while he is doing so you will have time to consider how many Dancers, and which ones, are eventually to live there. I am delighted!" And he shook hands with each of them in turn before taking his leave.

Muria took Lady Bethna to look at the dorters and the kitchens while Ruid took Lord Felsal on a tour of the other buildings. Lord Felsal wrote notes, took measurements, noted especially the type of flooring in the practice rooms, which buildings faced East and so forth. Then they went together to the Sanctuary. When they eventually gathered again in Muria's study, Lord Felsal was smiling like a child let loose in a toy-shop! He was clearly excited by the prospect of building a similar complex.

"I shall set my best architects to work on this as soon as we get home!" he exclaimed.

****

A year passed. Tiera danced once again in all the great Festivals of the year, celebrated another birthday, and moved into the senior group, along with all her year-mates. There had been a little ceremony, just as when she graduated from the beginners' class and became a Novice. Now she was a Neophyte, along with Selma and Bron, Nerron and Ambla, Jekka, Emmi, and all the others from their year.

In some of the afternoon classes they were encouraged to invent dances of their own, and apart from dancing they were now learning a great deal more about healing and about the power of crystals, though there would be another two years of training before they were considered fully-fledged Dancers.

Milon, Yssa and Lyria were in their final year of training so they were seldom in the same classes, though now that Tiera was a senior, too, their timetables were similar and they spent more time together. Muria, watching them together in the gardens, knew that their involvement in the drama of the Swathia mines had created a special bond between them in addition to their half-fairy blood.

Bron, watching from a different window, saw how Tiera leaned towards Milon, how her eyes were constantly on him, and had to resign himself to the fact that he would never gain Tiera's affection. Ever since the day he found her unconscious in the bushes, he had thought of himself as her protector and hoped that one day, when they were older, he might be more than that.

But since Tiera had discovered that she and Milon were both half-fay, he had feared that would never happen and now, since they had come back from Swathia, it was obvious that she had eyes for nobody but Milon.

He was startled by the pressure of a hand on his shoulder: Selma's. He brushed his hand across his eyes, embarrassed to be seen weeping.

"Bron, she'll always be your friend. You've had a very special place in her life, ever since the day we found her in the bushes."

"So have you," he retorted gruffly and hurried away, his head sunk between his shoulders.

****

"Have you thought about what you want to do when you've finished your training?" Yssa asked one day when all the half-fays were sitting on the lawn.

"I don't know," said Tiera, "I've still got time before I need to decide. What about you?"

"I've decided I want to serve the Temple as a priestess. I talked to Tama and Muria about it a while

264

back and they've arranged for me to spend a few days at the Temple very soon."

"Do you have any idea what you want to do, Milon?"

"I'd like to teach young dancers, like Ruid. I admire him and I'd like to be as much like him as possible."

"You and every boy at Dancers' Hall!" laughed his sister, "But that's no bad thing. There'll always be a need for men to dance and teach."

They could not have known that, at that very moment, their teachers were considering the very same question.

****

"I have had a message from Lord Felsal," Muria said to her assembled staff, "He says that the new Hall will be finished before long and he would like one of us to go out to Illia to supervise the equipping and furnishing of it. So, my dears, we can't put off any longer the business of deciding who will be in charge of the new Hall, and who else is to go with them."

Nobody spoke.

"Yes, I know it is going to be a tough decision. It has to be one of us four, as nobody else has sufficient experience. It obviously can't be myself - or, on the other hand, maybe it could! I could leave Ruid in charge here....."

"I'll go," said Tama quietly, "I like Lord Felsal and Lady Bethna, I liked what I saw of Illia." "Tama, that is wonderful. You have all the experience and all the skills it needs. Now, we must put our minds to the question of who goes with you."

"I have one suggestion," said Ruid, " I think we should ask Milon if he wants to go. His ambition is to teach, we were discussing it the other day, and it's important to have at least one male teacher in the new Hall."

"He's a bit too young to teach just yet. It's only a few weeks until he finishes his own training," said Allya.

"But Tama will be able to manage all the teaching to start with," Muria pointed out, "By the time more than one teacher is needed, Milon might well be old enough.

He could observe classes in the meantime, and maybe assist her a bit."

"Assuming Milon is willing, who else should we consider?" said Tama.

"If Milon goes, Tiera will want to go too," said Muria, "Have you seen them together?"

"Yes, but I'm not sure if it should be encouraged," said Allya, "They are so young."

"Young or not, I don't think we should separate them," said Muria quietly, "Let them grow up together, and they will find out naturally whether they are meant to be together as adults."

"Very well, we will ask them," said Tama, "As for the rest, may I make up a list of people I would like to take with me, and then ask them if they are willing?"

"That's an excellent idea. Make your list, and we'll proceed from there."

CHAPTER NINETEEN

Tiera was busy packing.

Everybody else in Blue Dorter was packing, too, but for Tiera it was different. Tomorrow, when most of the students left for the summer break, she would be leaving Dancers' Hall for ever and setting out for a new life in Illia. Tama had already gone ahead to finalise the arrangements at the new Hall, and tomorrow Lord Felsal's coaches would come to carry the rest of the new community of Dancers to join her.

Tiera was torn between excitement and regret; she was drawn to the adventure ahead and at the same time sad to leave the place where she had been so happy, the place that had become her true home and the good friends she had made there. To leave had been a difficult decision. When she'd been called to Muria's study and Tama asked if she would like to join the group going to the new Hall, she had said no, even when she knew that Milon would be one of the group. She had run to the furthest part of the garden and wept, until Selma found her lying on the grass, exhausted with sobbing.

"Don't you see, I can't go so far away and leave Dilla and Frol here in Allegria," she said, when Selma asked whatever was the matter, "Beatta is wonderful, she is so kind to them, but I am the only real family they have."

"Do you think it might be possible for them to go with you?"

Tiera stared at her. Such an idea had never entered her mind.

"Come on, let's go and find Muria and see what she thinks," said Selma, dragging Tiera to her feet.

"It might be possible," Muria conceded, once the two girls had poured out the idea, "We would have to talk to Tama about it, of course, and also to Lord Therron. Remember that Frol and Dilla are wards of court."

But Tama and Lord Therron had both been enthusiastic.

"It would be good to have some younger children with us," said Tama.

"But of course we can't separate this little family," said Lord Therron.

In the end, Beatta had asked if she could come too! Tama, when the idea of taking Dilla and Frol had been agreed upon, had tentatively put to her the idea that she might like to be Matron of the new Hall, and she had embraced the idea at once.

"Why, I like nothing better than looking after youngsters," she said.

"But we'll need to find somebody to take care of Dilla and Frol for a few weeks, because I will need you to travel with me, ahead of the Dancers, to help me set up the new Hall," said Tama.

"I'll ask my sister, Franca, the little ones know her well and she's almost as fond of them as I am," replied Beatta.

"I think we have found a second Cassie!" Tama had said to Muria when Beatta was out of earshot.

So now it was the very last day in Dancers' Hall, and Tiera's packing was almost finished. After she tucked Flip into her travelling bag, she extracted a rather similar dog from her closet and set off for Green

Dorter. As she expected, Crissa was there, packing like everybody else. Tiera took the dog from behind her back and said,

"I've brought you a goodbye present. I made him in craft classes."

Crissa stared at her, open mouthed, as she held the dog out, then said,

"But, didn't you know, I'm coming with you!"

Now it was Tiera's turn to stare. She had not heard Crissa's name mentioned in any of the many discussions about the new venture.

"No, I didn't know," she said.

"It was a last-minute decision," Crissa said, "There's nothing for me in Allegria. My parents have never thought of me as anything but a nuisance. They never really wanted any children and they were glad to send me to Dancers' Hall just to get me out of their way. Dancing means nothing to them. So I went to Muria and asked if I could be included in the party going to Illia and she said yes. Even Tama doesn't know yet."

"That's wonderful!" said Tiera, and they squashed

the plush dog between them as they hugged!

All the rest of that day there were goodbyes to be said, quite often tearfully. Tiera went to say goodbye to each of the teachers in turn, and thank them for everything they had taught her, and all that they had done for her in other ways, too.

Cassie crushed her in a bear-like hug and put a little parcel in her hand,

"Don't open it until you get there, my chick," she said.

Late in the afternoon, Tiera went to make her farewells to Muria, almost in tears before she got to her study, but Muria made her laugh by reminding her how she had arrived in the Dancer's midst and what a pathetic little scrap she had been.

"And look at you now. Another year and you will be a fully-fledged Dancer, and a fine one, too."

Now the tears really did spring to Tiera's eyes, and Muria's too. She had grown more fond of this half-fay child than she would like to admit, even to herself. So she embraced her and said,

"I will see all of you in the morning, of course,

before you leave."

That evening, Cassie made one of her most special feasts ever, and at the end Muria spoke about the new venture.

"This is a very special moment in the history of the Dancers, for there has only ever been one Dancers' Hall until now and apart from our duty to the Sacred Forest, our work has mainly benefited the people of Allegria. It feels right, and very exciting that another part of Kerran will have its own Dancers for healings and ceremonies, and, who knows, it is possible that there may in future be a Dancers' Hall in every province. But nothing will alter the fact that this is the Mother Hall, so to speak, and we will keep close links with all Dancers, wherever they might be. So, let us drink a toast to the new Hall, to Tama, and to the little group of Dancers who will set out tomorrow to join her."

****

After dinner, Tiera crept quietly out of the Hall and

made her way quickly down the gardens, through the gate and into the clearing, and sat down on the old log. She sent out her thoughts to the fairies:

"Lady Titania, Green Lord and dear Fairies, I have come to say goodbye."

Almost at once, she heard rustlings and saw the glimmer in the air that heralded their appearance, then they were all around her: the Queen and Lord of all the fairies, and a great crowd of fairies, elves and pixies. They stroked her hair, they patted her hand and, some of the more mischievous ones even tickled her feet!

"Not goodbye, dear Tiera. You will find us in the woodland wherever you go. We will always be there among the trees. Go now to Illia and you will find us there to meet you."

Then a hundred little hands pulled her from the log and somewhere a fairy piper began a tune.

"Dance with us, Tiera!".

So they spun and twirled in the moonlight, and Tiera was passed from one to another as they danced. Did she imagine it, or did the Green Lord himself briefly partner her? Then they were gone.

Tiera made her way back to bed with a light heart.

****

The morning dawned bright and fair, exactly the right weather for a journey. All over Dancers' Hall students heaved bags downstairs and along corridors. Parents and grandparents, uncles or aunts were waiting for many of them, but the chosen few who were setting out for Illia stood apart on the grass, waiting for Lord Felsal's carriages to arrive. Tiera found Dilla and Frol among them, holding Franca's hands rather tightly. Then Selma ran up to them while her mother called impatiently by the gate.

"Goodbye, dear Tiera. Promise you will write. Tell me everything that happens, she sniffed between sobs.

"Goodbye Selma," sobbed Tiera, "You've been the very best friend anyone could have. Of course I'll write, every time there's a messenger coming to Allegria. And look after Bron, please."

Selma nodded and ran to join her mother. Tiera noticed that she was blushing as she ran and was glad. "I think Selma and Bron have always belonged together," she thought, "I got in the way of that, so it is good that I am going away and leaving them here without me."

Now there was a rumbling of heavy wheels, and everyone moved towards the gate expecting Lord Felsal's carriages, but in the roadway outside the main gate, was a coach bearing Lord Therron's insignia. Out of it climbed Lord Therron who looked around for Muria, saw her talking to the waiting group of travellers and came across to her.

"Good morning, First Dancer," he said, "Do you know when Lord Felsal's carriages will be here?"

"They are due any minute, Lord Therron," Muria replied.

"Good. I have something for your Dancers to take with them, a gift for the new Dancers' Hall."

As they walked towards his coach, the carriages arrived, exactly as expected, followed by a covered cart to take the luggage. Lord Therron gathered the little group of Dancers round him and beckoned to the two footmen who were lifting a heavy bundle out of his coach. He folded back a corner of the cloth that covered it.

The Dancers all gasped in amazement - it was the beautiful amethyst geode that Lord Wilkin had found on the fateful day in the mine.

"There has always been a geode in the Sanctuary of your Hall, so I feel it is right that you take one with you to your new home."

Now Lord Felsal's men were loading bags and bundles into the cart, but the geode, too precious to travel with the luggage, was lifted with the greatest care into the leading carriage. With a last round of hugs and farewells, they clambered into the carriages, Tiera with Dilla and Frol, Verla, Nerron, Milon, Lenna and Zoran, Serra and last of all, Crissa. They had to squeeze up a little as the precious geode took up all the front bench of one coach, but nobody minded that because it was so wonderful to be taking it with them.

Then the drivers cracked their whips and slowly the carriages began to inch forward. Leaning out of the window, Tiera waved and waved as the Hall which had been her home and the teachers who had nurtured her grew smaller and smaller. Then the carriage rounded a bend and at last they were out of sight. Tiera pulled up the window and sat down next to her brother and sister as the wheels turned faster, carrying them towards a new life.

THE END.

THE STORY CONTINUES!

Follow Tiera's adventures as she discovers new gifts and finds both friends and enemies in Illia.

Find out more about her brother and sister as Dilla and Frol adjust to life at the new Dancers' Hall. What happens when Dilla runs into danger? How does Tiera save her life?

All this and much, much more in

DREAMDANCER

the second book in the series.